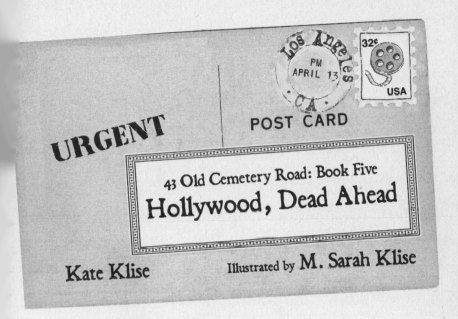

URGENT

POST CARD

Los Angeles
PM
APRIL 13
CA

32¢
USA

43 Old Cemetery Road: Book Five
Hollywood, Dead Ahead

Kate Klise   Illustrated by M. Sarah Klise

Houghton Mifflin Harcourt
Boston   New York

www.hmhco.com

The Library of Congress has cataloged the hardcover edition as follows:
Klise, Kate.
Hollywood, dead ahead / Kate Klise ; illustrated by M. Sarah Klise.
pages cm. — (43 Old Cemetery Road ; book 5)
Summary: When film producer Moe Block Busters offers to make their book into a movie,
Iggy, Olive, and Seymour head to Hollywood, where Olive, furious at being written out of the script,
enlists the help of a famed femme fatale to scare the despicable director half to death.
[1. Letters—Fiction. 2. Motion pictures—Production and direction—Fiction.
3. Ghosts—Fiction. 4. Actors and actresses—Fiction.
5. Hollywood (Los Angeles, Calif.)—Fiction.
6. Humorous stories.] I. Klise, M. Sarah, illustrator. II. Title.
PZ7.K684Hol 2013
[Fic]—dc23
2013003922

ISBN 978-0-547-85283-6 hardcover
ISBN 978-0-544-33661-2 paperback

Designed by M. Sarah Klise

Manufactured in United States of America
DOC 10 9 8 7 6 5 4 3 2 1
4500491975

You grow up the day you have your first real laugh—at yourself.

Ethel Barrymore

Welcome to 43 Old Cemetery Road!

That's the address of Spence Mansion. It's also the title of a book by . . .

Olive C. Spence

Ignatius
B. Grumply

with illustrations
by their adopted son,
Seymour Hope.

Their book is an international bestseller!

Fans all around the world
eagerly await the new chapters
of 43 Old Cemetery Road,
which arrive by mail every few months.

(That's as fast as Ignatius, Olive, and Seymour can create them.)

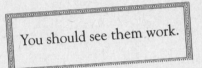

You should see them work.

Ignatius likes to write in his bedroom
on the second floor.

Seymour draws in his studio
on the third floor.

And Olive does her best editing
in the cupola.

They all meet in the dining room for meals and to read their fan mail. This is where many business discussions take place.

And speaking of business, there's none of that. *Speaking*, that is. Why not?

Because there's a rule at Spence Mansion. It's strictly enforced.

All Business Must Be Discussed in Writing.

That way, no one's opinion gets left out because of age, gender, or the fact that one member of this family (Olive) is a ghost who can communicate only through the written word.

There's another rule at Spence Mansion.
It's also strictly enforced.

Majority Rules.

That means whenever an important business decision must be made,
if all three residents of Spence Mansion can't agree on what to do,
they do whatever *two* residents want to do.

It's because of these two rules that we can share with you
the following story,
which is still spoken about
in hushed whispers
in Hollywood.

The whole thing began with
—what else?—
a letter,
which has been reprinted in its entirety
on the pages that follow.

MOE BLOCK BUSTERS
BUSTER BOY ENTERTAINMENT

630 WEST 5TH STREET, LOS ANGELES, CA 90071
TEL: 555-IMA-STAR

March 2

OVERNIGHT MAIL

Ignatius B. Grumply
43 Old Cemetery Road
Ghastly, Illinois

Dear Mr. Grumply,

I am a big fan of your book. But then again, who isn't? I won't beat around the bush, old boy. I want to make a movie of *43 Old Cemetery Road*.

I own the biggest studio in Hollywood. I'm sure you've seen my films: *Sharks, Return of the Sharks, Explosions, Explosions 2,* and *Sharks, Explosions, Bathing Beauties, and Werewolves!*

In my fifty years of producing movies, I've never had a flop. I know the formula for making blockbusters, and I know your story would be a huge hit. How can we lose? We take your bestselling book, add a cute kid, and throw in a fabulous femme fatale with one foot in the grave. I can already smell the Academy Award!

Give me a call so we can iron out the details. I can't wait to get you to Hollywood, old boy.

Reach for the stars!

Moe Block Busters

Moe Block Busters
Founder & President
Buster Boy Entertainment

MBB/mm

43 Old Cemetery Road
Third Floor
Ghastly, Illinois

March 3

Dear Iggy and Olive,

I couldn't resist opening the letter from California. We HAVE to do this! Please????? <u>Explosions 2</u> is my all-time favorite movie. Or it would be if Iggy would let me see it.

Can you imagine the biggest producer in Hollywood making a movie about us? It would be the coolest thing <u>ever</u>. Olive, I know you probably don't like movies. I bet they didn't even exist when you were alive. But trust me, they're GREAT!

I made a ballot for this business decision. Please cast your vote!

Love,

— Seymour

P.S. What's a femme fatale?

10.

Should we go to Hollywood
and become movie stars?

☒ Yes
☐ No

Should we go to Hollywood
and become movie stars?

☐ Yes
☐ No

Should we go to Hollywood
and become movie stars?

☐ Yes
☐ No

IGNATIUS B. GRUMPLY

A WRITER IN RESIDENCE

March 3

Seymour Hope
Third floor
43 Old Cemetery Road
Ghastly, Illinois

Dear Seymour,

The expression *femme fatale* is French for "deadly woman." It's a phrase you hear often in film studies. A femme fatale is a character who uses her feminine charms in mysterious ways to achieve hidden purposes.

But never mind that. I have no intention of allowing Moe Block Busters to make a movie about us. I've had the misfortune of seeing some of his films. To say they're a waste of time and money doesn't begin to descri

Oh, Iggy! Isn't it exciting?

Olive, you're here. I thought you were ru

I was running errands. I got home just a moment ago and saw the mail on the dining room table. Imagine—a film about us!

12.

Don't get your hopes up, Olive. Moe Block Busters might be the biggest producer in Hollywood, but only because he makes the most dreadful films. The man doesn't have an original thought in his head.

But darling, *we* can provide that. Just think. We'll be movie stars.

Forgive me, Olive, but have you ever seen a movie?

You and Seymour seem to forget that I was alive until 1911. Moving pictures were created in this country in the 1890s. You've heard of Thomas Edison, haven't you?

The inventor of the light bulb? Of course.

Well, Mr. Edison also invented a Kinetoscope, a device that enabled people to watch short films. That was in 1891. He also patented a motion picture camera called the Kinetograph. The rest is history.

I had no idea. What were movies like in your day?

Silent, for one thing. But no one minded because the films were fabulous!

Then you'd be disappointed by the movies made today. They're dull, predictable, and usually rated

R for racy, repugnant, and ridiculous. Trust me, Olive. You wouldn't want Moe Block Busters to make a movie about us.

But Iggy, it's *our* story. How could it be anything but wonderful?

Because that's how Hollywood works. I've heard too many horror stories from fellow writers. Mr. Busters would take our idea, mangle it into something we wouldn't recognize, and then burp it up for mass consumption.

Good heavens! When did you become so vulgar and cynical?

I'm sorry. I just feel strongly that this is something we shouldn't do.

Oh, do you? Because Seymour and I feel strongly that this is something we *should* do. Two against one. Majority rules.

I see.

Furthermore, I've always believed that I was born for the big screen. And I'm pleased to know that Hollywood's most successful producer recognizes that I'm a fabulous femme fatale, even though I might have one foot in the grave. Or two.

But I have no acting experience. And my face could stop a clock.

Nonsense, Iggy! You're as handsome as any leading man. Besides, I'll be the star of the film. I've heard our fans say that I'm the most colorful character.

Olive, you're invisible.

Yes, but I have a closet full of gowns I've been dying to wear for decades.

So I guess we're doing this.

Oh, don't look so glum. We're going to be *movie stars*. Is that so terrible?

I don't like the idea, but maybe we'll get some good material out of it for the book.

There you go! Please call Moe Block Busters, dear.

I will after I take a nap. These business discussions always exhaust me.

Nap? There's no time for a *nap*. Call Mr. Busters now—before he changes his mind!

❧THE GHASTLY TIMES❧

Wednesday, March 4
Cliff Hanger, Editor

"We're Living in Ghastly Times"

50 cents
Morning Edition

Hollywood, Here They Come!

They promise they're not leaving Ghastly forever—just long enough to go to Hollywood and become movie stars.

That's the news from Spence Mansion, where Ignatius B. Grumply, Olive C. Spence and Seymour Hope are packing their bags and preparing for the trip of a lifetime after receiving an offer from Moe Block Busters, Hollywood's most successful filmmaker, to produce a movie based on *43 Old Cemetery Road*. (See story below.)

"I don't know how this will turn out," said the ever-modest and often grumpy Grumply. "If it were up to me, we'd stay home and continue working on our book."

But Grumply lost the vote to Hope and Spence.

"I cannot wait to go," said Hope. "If Mr. Busters makes a movie about us, my dad will have to let me watch it, no matter what it's rated. Right, Iggy?"

Grumply was noncommittal. "We'll cross that bridge when we come to it," he

The bestselling trio is
heading to Hollywood.

said. "Let's just hope we're back here in time for your birthday."

Seymour Hope will turn twelve on April 13, the same day the creators of *43 Old Cemetery Road* have promised their readers three new chapters of their bestselling book. Judging by Grumply's sour mood, it seems clear the trio hasn't started the next installment.

Producer Predicts "Sure-Fire Hit"

Moe Block Busters invented the
blockbuster movie.

Moe Block Busters says that it's a no-brainer.

"I've been making movies long enough to know a blockbuster when I see one," said Busters in a telephone interview from Los Angeles. "And this is a sure-fire hit. You take a terrific story, add a cute kid and throw in a woman who has 'screen legend' written all over her. I'm telling you right now that *43 Old Cemetery Road* will be the most successful ghost movie in history.

Continued on page 2, column 1

PRODUCER *Continued from page 1, column 2*

It's what we in the industry call an instant classic."

Mr. Busters said designers are already building a replica of Spence Mansion in Hollywood.

"As much as I'd love to film *43 Old Cemetary Road* in Ghastly, it'll be easier to shoot here," said Busters. "Plus, it'll be cheaper. You've got to keep your eye on the bottom line if you want to make money in this business."

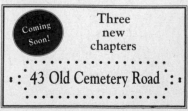
Who Will Care for Spence Mansion?

Briss says he can fix anything.

While a movie based on *43 Old Cemetery Road* is filmed on a Hollywood set, who will care for the real Spence Mansion in Ghastly?

"I will," said Hugh Briss, Ghastly's newest resident.

Briss, owner of Home Sweet Home Repairs, has been hired by Ignatius B. Grumply to make a few repairs at Spence Mansion.

"I gave Mr. Briss a list of things I'd like done around the house," said Grumply. "Nothing major. Just a few leaky faucets, a mole problem and a minor roof repair."

Briss predicted he'll have the to-do list completed within a day or two. "I can fix this stuff with one hand tied behind my back," Briss bragged.

Asked if he was concerned about making repairs to a haunted house, Briss laughed. "The only scary thing about this job is how much money I'll make. Mr. Grumply has promised me five hundred bucks. This'll be a cakewalk!"

Briss will not be responsible for Spence Mansion's resident dog and cats.

"I've offered to feed and walk the pets," said M. Balm, chief librarian at the Ghastly Public Library. "The only thing I ask in return is that Seymour keep us posted on all the news from Hollywood."

"I'll write home every chance I get," Hope promised.

Balm suggested the boy send his letters to the *Ghastly Times*. "That way, everyone can enjoy reading them," said Balm.

MOE BLOCK BUSTERS
BUSTER BOY ENTERTAINMENT

630 WEST 5TH STREET, LOS ANGELES, CA 90071
TEL: 555-IMA-STAR

March 4

Ignatius B. Grumply
43 Old Cemetery Road
Ghastly, Illinois

Dear Ignatius,

What a thrill to talk with you on the telephone yesterday! I feel like I've
known you forever, old boy.

I've asked my assistant, Myra Manes, to send you a contract so we can
get this show on the road. It's just a simple legal document that gives us
permission to turn your book into a movie.

I'll also have Myra send plane tickets. The sooner you can get out here,
the better. Let's not lose momentum, old boy!

Reach for the stars!

Moe Block Busters

Moe Block Busters
Founder & President
Buster Boy Entertainment

MBB/mm

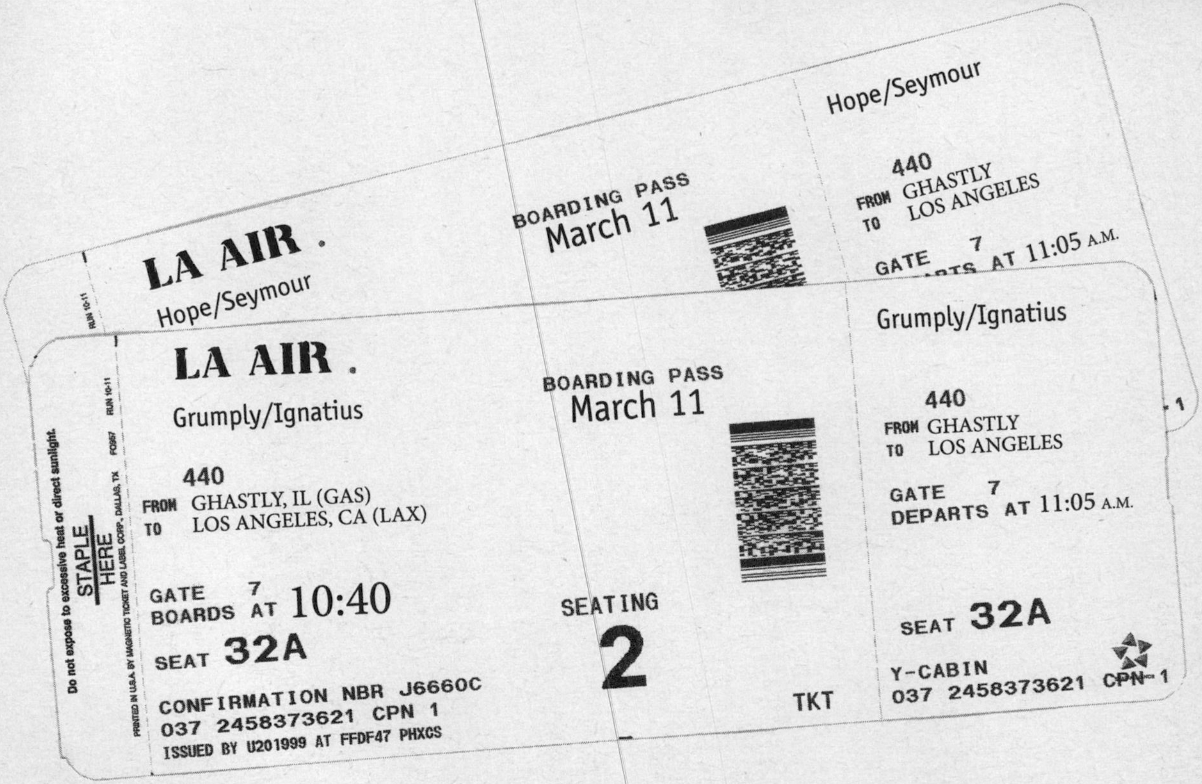
LA AIR
Hope/Seymour
BOARDING PASS
March 11
Hope/Seymour
440
FROM GHASTLY
TO LOS ANGELES
GATE 7
AT 11:05 A.M.
LA AIR
Grumply/Ignatius
440
FROM GHASTLY, IL (GAS)
TO LOS ANGELES, CA (LAX)
GATE 7
BOARDS AT 10:40
SEAT 32A
CONFIRMATION NBR J6660C
037 2458373621 CPN 1
ISSUED BY U201999 AT FFDF47 PHXCS
BOARDING PASS
March 11
SEATING
2
TKT
Grumply/Ignatius
440
FROM GHASTLY
TO LOS ANGELES
GATE 7
DEPARTS AT 11:05 A.M.
SEAT 32A
Y-CABIN
037 2458373621 CPN 1
Do not expose to excessive heat or direct sunlight.
STAPLE HERE
PRINTED IN U.S.A. BY MAGNETIC TICKET AND LABEL CORP., DALLAS, TX
FO957
RUN 10-11

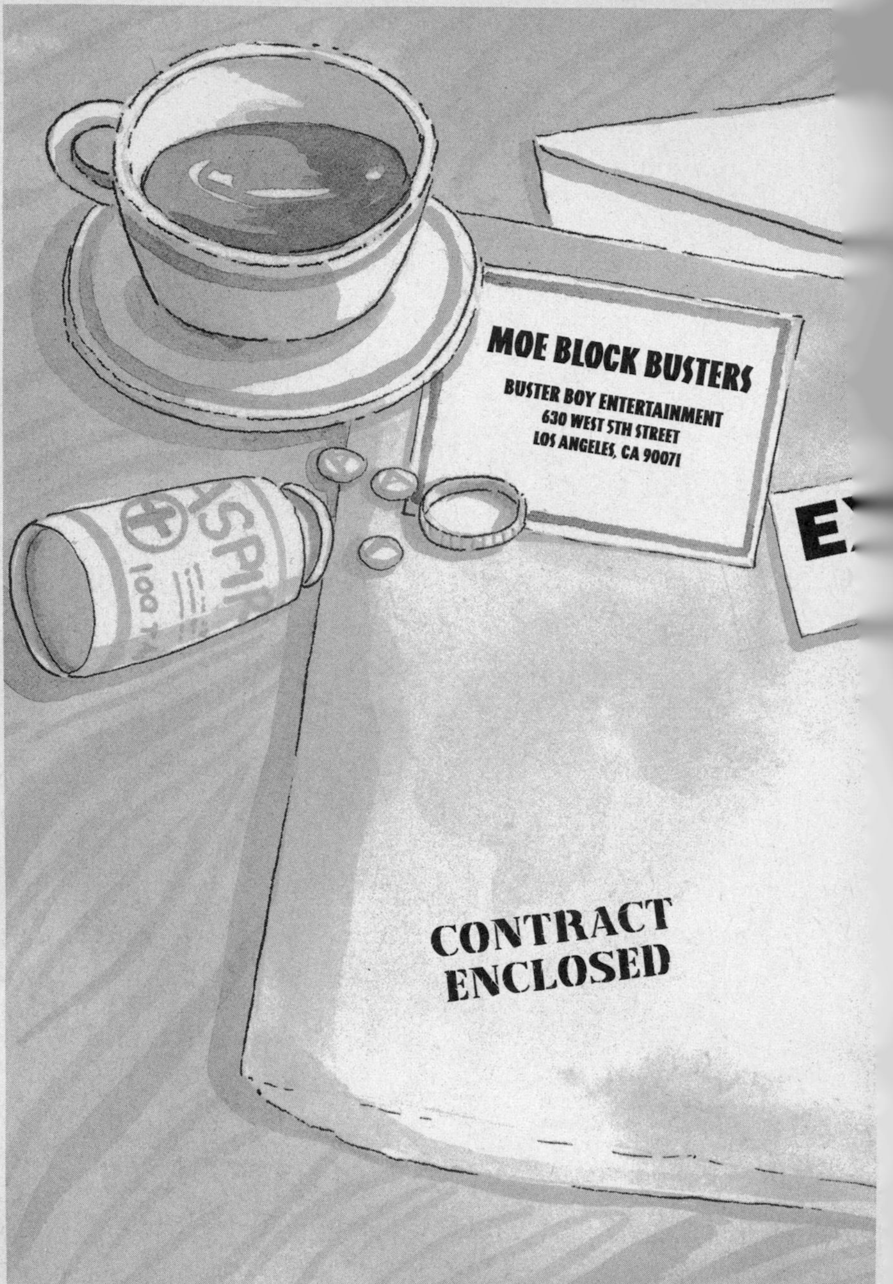
MOE BLOCK BUSTERS
BUSTER BOY ENTERTAINMENT
630 WEST 5TH STREET
LOS ANGELES, CA 90071
CONTRACT
ENCLOSED

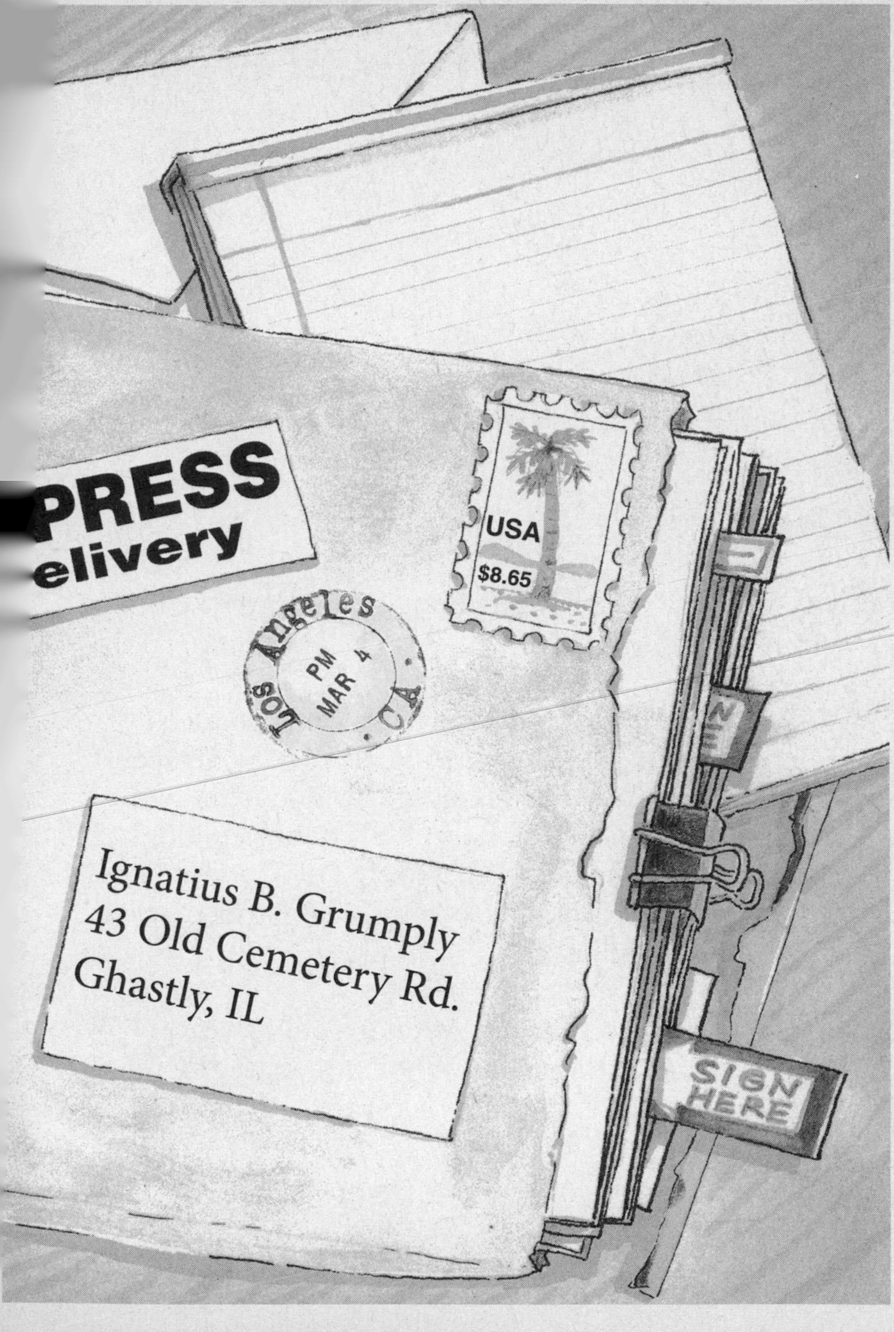
PRESS
elivery
USA
$8.65
Los Angeles
PM
MAR 4
CA
Ignatius B. Grumply
43 Old Cemetery Rd.
Ghastly, IL
SIGN
HERE

IGNATIUS B. GRUMPLY

A WRITER IN RESIDENCE

43 OLD CEMETERY ROAD   **2ND FLOOR**   **GHASTLY, ILLINOIS**

March 6

Moe Block Busters
Buster Boy Entertainment
630 W. 5th Street
Los Angeles, CA 90071

Dear Mr. Busters,

I received the 429-page contract. I'd hardly call it a
simple document.

I'm still reviewing the fine print, but I've already
found one big mistake on the last page of the contract. My name alone is listed. I understand why
Seymour's name isn't there. He's not old enough to
sign legal documents. But surely Olive should be a
signatory. Will you please send a new contract with
Olive's name added?

As for the plane tickets, there are only two: one for
me and one for Seymour. When you send the new
contract, kindly include a ticket for Olive so tha

Iggy, it's fine. I'll meet you there.

What? Why?

I'm not ready. Go to Hollywood without me. I'll catch up with you later.

Olive, have you read the contract? I can't make heads or tails of it.

Oh, just sign the silly thing, Iggy. They want to make a movie of our book. How complicated can it be?

Very, apparently. I can't figure out if we're even being paid for this.

I'm sure we'll get paid after we finish making the movie. Moe Block Busters seems like a very trustworthy man.

You just like him because he described you as a screen legend.

That's part of it. The other reason is because Seymour is over the moon. Do you hear him singing in his room? Don't ruin this for him by nit-picking every comma in the contract.

You really don't mind that your name isn't on it?

Heavens, no. The biggest movie stars always have other people handle the paperwork.

Olive, you're not a movie star yet.

I know, but just wait till my fans see my opera glasses on the big screen. Now stop scowling and start signing. Here's a pen. Write your name neatly so it's one hundred percent legal.

Done. Now I'll have to write another letter to Mr. Busters without your commentary.

Oh, just send him this letter. He already knows about me from reading our book. And because he'll be reading these very words, might I add, Mr. Busters, that I am ready for my close-up?

On that note, I'll sign off.

Me too.

Sincerely,

Ignatius B. Grumply

and Olive C. Spence

MOE BLOCK BUSTERS
BUSTER BOY ENTERTAINMENT

630 WEST 5TH STREET, LOS ANGELES, CA 90071

TEL: 555-IMA-STAR

March 9

Ignatius B. Grumply
43 Old Cemetery Road
Ghastly, Illinois

Dear Ignatius,

I knew you were a talented writer, but your letter has me laughing my head off! Genius, that's what you are, old boy!

Wish I'd discovered you fifty years ago when I was at the beginning of my career rather than the end. No matter. I'll see you soon.

Reaching for the stars—and pretty sure I've found one.

Moe Block Busters

Moe Block Busters
Founder & President
Buster Boy Entertainment

MBB/mm

I. B. Grumply
43 Old Cemetery Road
Ghastly, Illinois

Moe Block Busters
Buster Boy Entertainment
630 W. 5th Street
71

429.

IN WITNESS WHEREOF, the parties hereto have
fully executed this Agreement and are forever committed to the terms outlined herein.

Ignatius
B. Grumply
Ignatius B. Grumply
Creator, 43 Old Cemetery Road

Moe Block Busters
Moe Block Busters
Buster Boy Entertainment

SIGN
HERE

Myra—
Schedule a
press
conference
ASAP! MBB

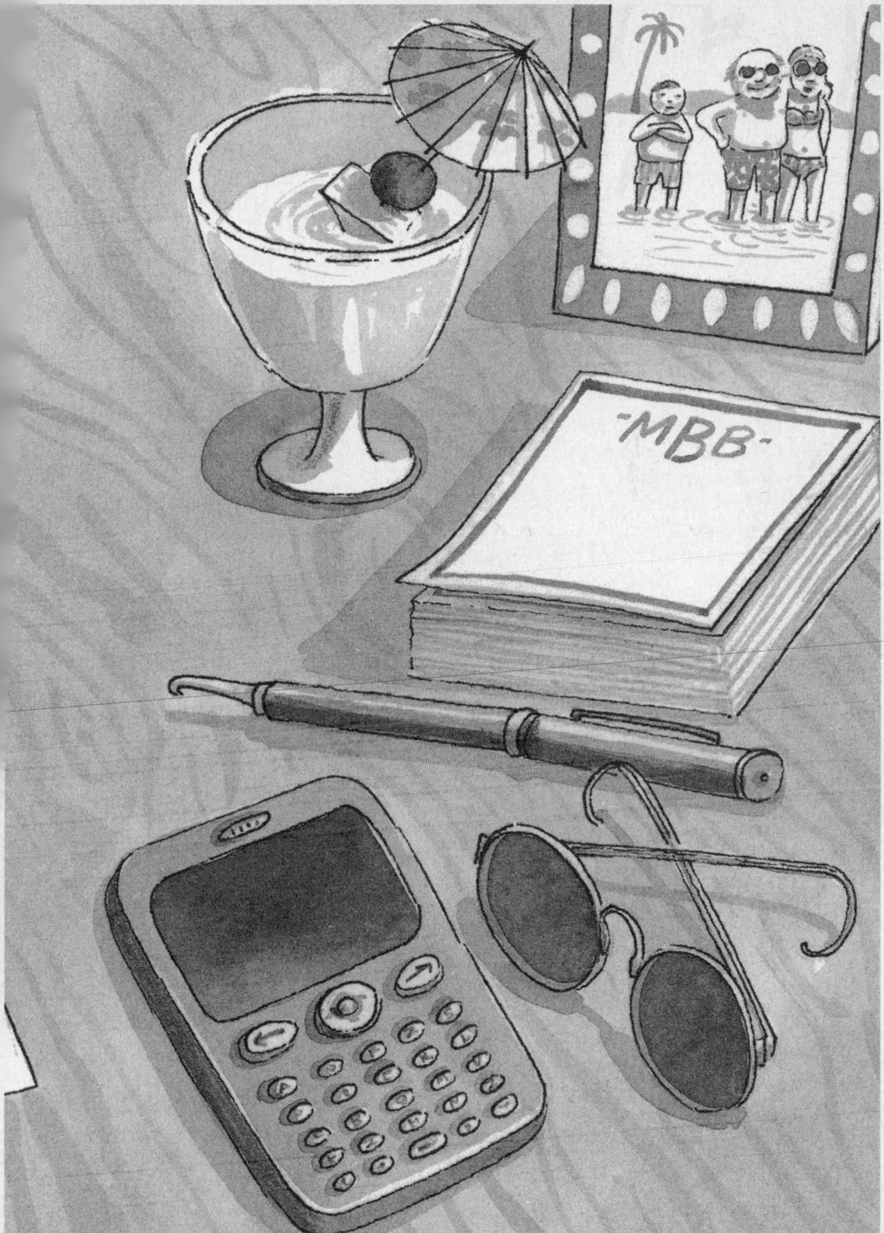
-MBB-

THE HOLLYWOOD WHISPER

Wednesday, March 11   "Movie News and Secrets You're Just *Dying* to Hear" $1.50

"I Own Olive!"
Buster Boy Entertainment Buys *43 Old Cemetery Road*

In a move Hollywood watchers are calling the deal of the century, Buster Boy Entertainment has purchased all rights to the bestselling ghost story *43 Old Cemetery Road*.

"I own Olive!" announced Moe Block Busters, founder and president of Buster Boy Entertainment, at a press conference yesterday.

According to Busters, his studio now owns the entire *43 Old Cemetery Road* brand. "That includes anything that has been written, is being written now or will be written about Spence Mansion and the characters who live there, along with T-shirts, trinkets, video games, pajamas and hoodies based on the brand," Busters explained. "It's a heckuva contract."

The contract also includes rights to a new character called Evilo. "Little old lady ghosts are too quiet, too boring for today's movie audiences," Busters explained. "So we're launching

Busters (left) relies on Manes (right) for all his big deals.

a new character called Evilo. That's Olive spelled backwards. The first film in the series will be about a ghost named Evilo who haunts an old house and the father and son who try to get rid of her. I'm calling it *Evilo Must Go!*"

Busters said the movie will be written and directed by Phillip D. Rubbish. Production is scheduled to begin later this month.

Rubbish Rises to the Top

Rubbish will run Buster Boy studio for one month.

Phillip D. Rubbish is known for his snazzy special effects and creative camera moves. But could Rubbish's next move be to the head office of Buster Boy Entertainment?

"I'm ready to retire," said Moe Block Busters at yesterday's press conference. "I just have to find someone to take over my movie studio."

Many Hollywood insiders thought

Continued on page 2, column 1

RUBBISH *Continued from page 1, column 2*

Busters would ask Myra Manes, his trusted adviser, to succeed him. "Myra's a smart cookie," Busters said. "That gal writes the most creative contracts in Hollywood. But she's not ruthless enough to run a Hollywood studio. Phillip D. Rubbish is another story."

Rubbish, who got his start as a tabloid reporter in London, freely admits to having clawed his way to the top at Buster Boy Entertainment. "I'll steal a script, tap a telephone and double-cross a body double—all before breakfast," he said in his roguish British accent.

But what does Rubbish know about running a film studio?

"Plenty," Rubbish replied. "I know the Buster Boy recipe for success. And I'm telling you right now, *Evilo Must Go!* is going to be a movie to die for. To die for!"

Busters has given Rubbish full authority to run his studio during the production of *Evilo Must Go!* After yesterday's press conference, Busters left by private plane for a month-long vacation in the Caribbean.

"Knock 'em dead, Rubbish," Busters said with a wink before stepping into his private plane. "Oh, and if you need anything, ask Myra Manes. She's my go-to gal."

Ivana Oscar Will Star in *Evilo Must Go!*

A young Oscar (left) dazzled fans before she retired (right).

Screen legend Ivana Oscar, 92, has agreed to come out of retirement to play the role of an evil ghost in *Evilo Must Go!*

Oscar, known to fans as Hollywood's favorite femme fatale, has starred in more than a hundred films during a career that spans seven decades. The actress, who retired to Florida thirty years ago, said her decision to return to Hollywood was based on a call she received from Moe Block Busters.

"He promised me I'll win an Academy Award if I play this role," said Oscar from her home in Florida. "It's the only award I have left to win before I die."

Oscar admitted she hasn't read the script yet. "I didn't read my contract, either. When you're my age, you don't want to waste time reading 600-page contracts. Besides, I've been too busy reading *43 Old Cemetery Road.* What a hoot!"

Miss Oscar is expected to arrive in Los Angeles on Friday afternoon.

CASTING CALL

Looking for male actors between the ages of 10 and 18 to audition for the role of Sylvester, an earnest boy whose home is haunted by a hideous ghost named Evilo.

Le Beverly Hills Hotel
"Where the Stars Stay in Style"
444 N. Rexford Drive
Beverly Hills, CA 90210

March 11

Olive C. Spence
43 Old Cemetery Road
Ghastly, Illinois

Dear Olive,

Don't come. There's been a huge mistake. And no,
I'm not going to say I told you so. This is entirely
my fault for signing that ridiculous contract.

I'll explain everything when I get home. It may
take several days to undo this legal knot, but I've
already put in a call to Mr. Busters's assistant,
Myra Manes. That's the first step. Then I'll have
to think of a way to make this up to Seymour. He's
disappointed that he's not going to be a movie star.
I suspect you'll be disappointed, too.

I'll write a longer letter soon, but I want to get
this off in today's mail so you know *not* to come to
California.

With love and apologies, Iggy

O.C.S.
Ghost Writer in Residence
43 Old Cemetery Road, The Cupola
Ghastly, Illinois

March 11

Ignatius B. Grumply
c/o Le Beverly Hills Hotel
444 N. Rexford Drive
Beverly Hills, CA 90210

Dear Iggy,

I'm so excited to see you in Hollywood! Please meet me at the Los Angeles airport on Friday afternoon at four o'clock.

I've mailed a few things in advance. I feel it's unbecoming for a star of my caliber to carry her own bags. Kindly tell the hotel concierge to take my luggage to my suite. I'm assuming I'll be in the penthouse. The gowns should be hung carefully on padded hangers. I'll unpack the rest when I arrive.

Oh, and will you please tell Moe Block Busters that I'm bringing my own wardrobe? I know there are marvelous costume designers in Hollywood, but they can't top my vintage Victorian gowns.

See you soon, darling! Give my love to Seymour.

Olive

P.S. I shall wait for you inside the airport, Iggy. I'll be wearing a pink feather boa and tinted opera glasses.

P.P.S. I know I could travel more quickly in my ghostly fashion, but I want to make an entrance, just like a *real* movie star.

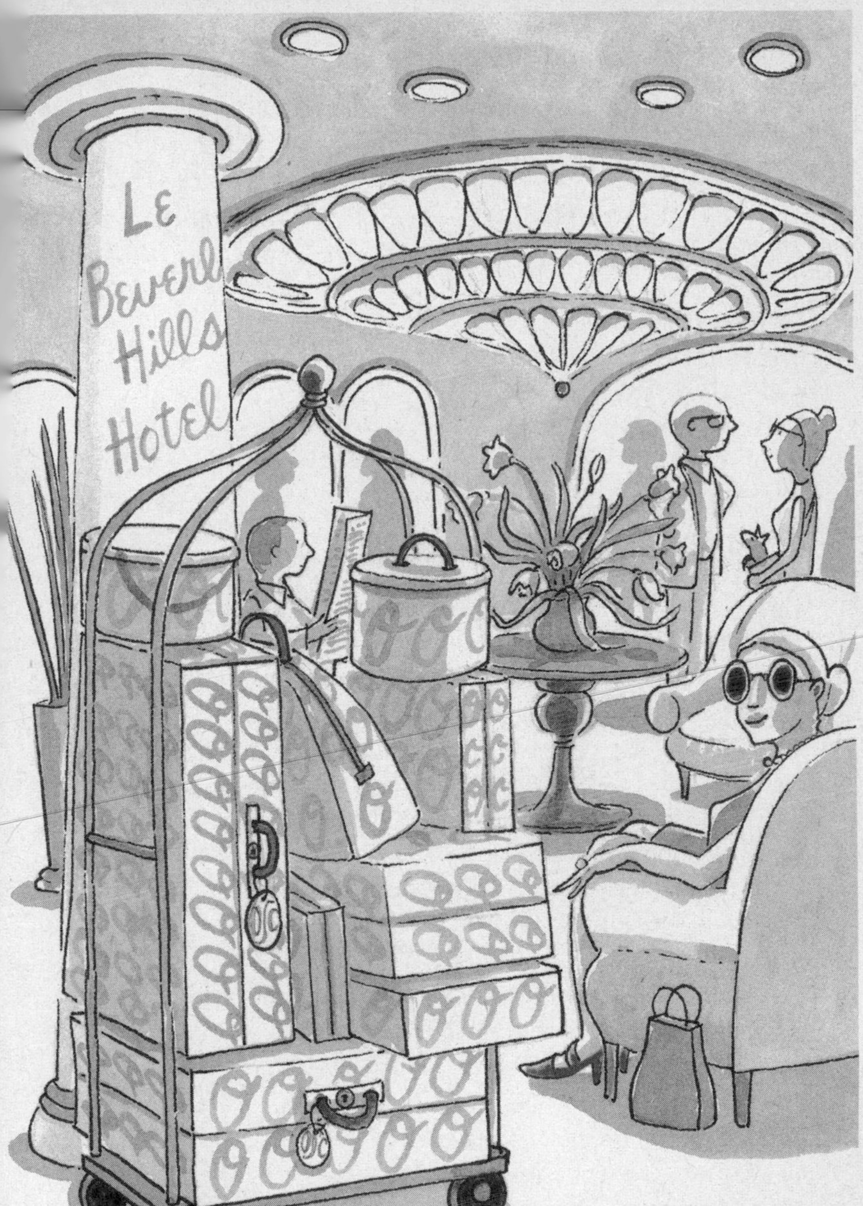
Le Beverl Hills Hotel

MYRA MANES

PERSONAL ADVISER & ASSISTANT TO MOE BLOCK BUSTERS

BUSTER BOY ENTERTAINMENT

630 WEST 5TH STREET   LOS ANGELES, CA 90071

Delivered by Courier

March 12

Ignatius B. Grumply
c/o Le Beverly Hills Hotel
444 N. Rexford Drive
Beverly Hills, CA 90210

Dear Mr. Grumply,

I received your phone message. I'm sorry you're not happy
with the terms of the contract, but that's something you
should've considered before you signed your name to a legally
binding document.

As the creator of *43 Old Cemetery Road,* you effectively transferred all your rights to Buster Boy Entertainment when you
signed that contract. It is entirely legal and enforceable in a court
of law. No other name—and certainly not that of an imaginary
coauthor—is required on the contract.

Forgive me if I sound rude, Mr. Grumply. Your "ghost story"
might play well with young readers, but you're with the big
boys now in Hollywood. They believe in nothing except power.

Regarding the question of payment: There is no compensation
clause in the contract. Your payment is the privilege of seeing
your book made into a major motion picture.

There is nothing more to be said on the matter unless you want Buster Boy Entertainment to sue you for breach of contract. If you'll turn to page 322 of your contract, you'll see that you and Seymour are required to have makeovers within 72 hours of arriving in Los Angeles.

I took the liberty of setting up appointments for you. Luke Ahtmee is expecting you at nine o'clock on Friday morning.

Helpfully yours,

Myra Manes

Myra Manes

P.S. You'll like Luke. He's my personal hairdresser.

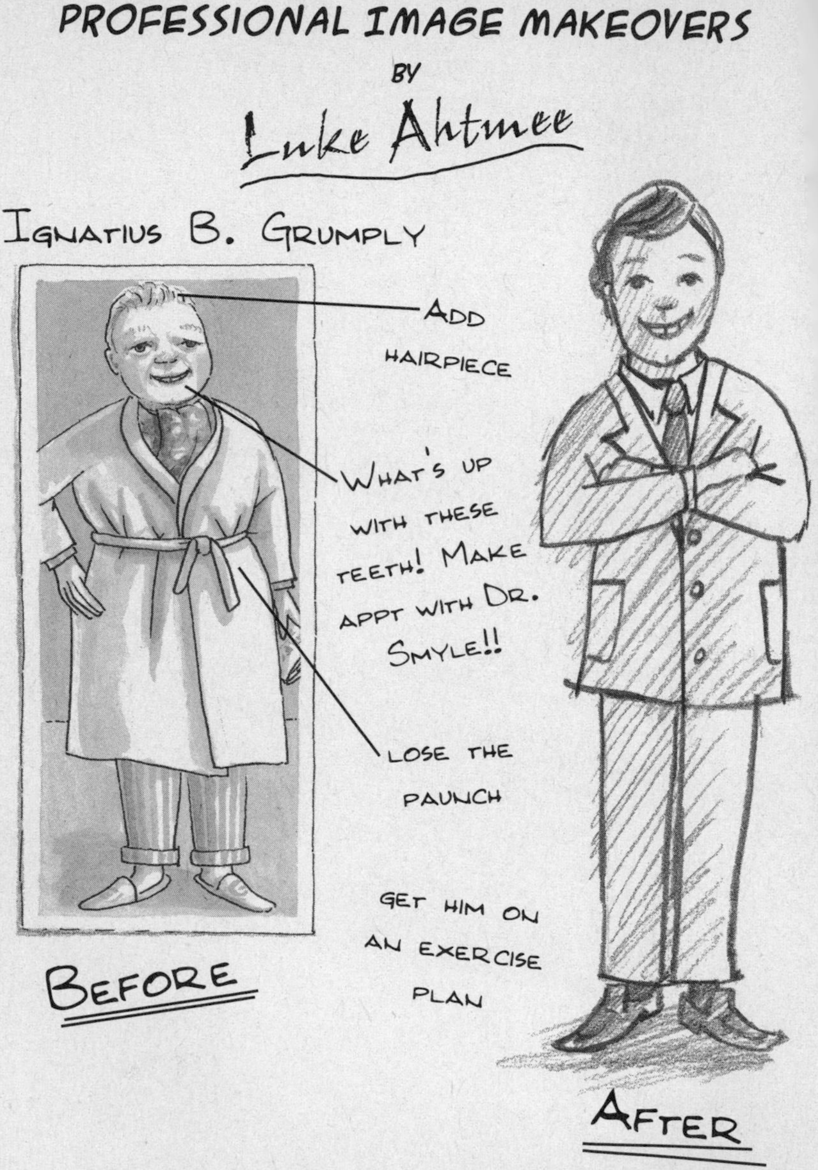
PROFESSIONAL IMAGE MAKEOVERS
BY
Luke Ahtmee
Ignatius B. Grumply
Add hairpiece
What's up with these teeth! Make appt with Dr. Smyle!!
lose the paunch
get him on an exercise plan
Before
After

Seymour Hope

ADD SUNGLASSES

CUT HAIR!

APPLY PRODUCT

LESS CHILDREN'S BOOK CHARACTER

MORE ROCK STAR

DOES HE NEED A NEW ATTITUDE?

SOMETHING EDGIER?

AFTER

Le Beverly Hills Hotel

"Where the Stars Stay in Style"

444 N. Rexford Drive
Beverly Hills, CA 90210

March 13

Dear Olive,

I just received your letter. I'm not sure which room you're in. As always, it will be easier for you to find me than it will be for me to find you. In any case, I'm terribly sorry I wasn't able to meet your plane. Seymour and I have spent the entire day with a man named Luke Ahtmee, who insi

I'm not speaking to you.

Olive! You're here! I'm so relieved to know you made it safely from the airport.

I took a taxi. It was awful.

I'm sorry. Were you able to check in?

The hotel is full. There are no rooms available, and there is no reservation in my name.

Ugh. I was afraid of that.

And I can't find my luggage. Not a piece of it.

We'll track it down, Olive. Don't worry.

Oh, Iggy. You can't imagine the day I've had. At the airport this morning, I set off every alarm known to man, woman, or ghost. When I finally got on the plane, every seat was taken except one. I squeezed in, but then a slovenly creature eating an enormous ham sandwich sat on top of me. So I had to stand for the *entire* flight. And no one offered me a morsel to eat—or even a cup of tea!

Air travel isn't what it used to be.

When we finally landed in Los Angeles, I waited and waited for you inside the airport. But you never showed up. I eventually drifted outside, where I found a shiny black limousine waiting at the curb. Curious spectators were gathered around with cameras. Naturally, I assumed they were waiting for me. So I smiled like the shy star I am, tossed my feather boa over one shoulder, and strode gracefully toward the magnificent car. But right when I was about to get in, a decrepit old bat pushed past me and got into the car. You should've heard the applause! I have no idea who the woman was or why everyone thought *she* was so important. But off she went, in *my* limousine. I finally hailed a taxi. The driver was beyond rude and the back seat smelled like I don't know what. And then . . . Iggy, you're not even *listening* to me!

Of course I am, Olive.

No, you're not. You're staring at yourself in the mirror.

Can't I do both? What do you think of my new look?

In a word? Ridiculous.

Quite a change, isn't it? I can't decide if I like it. I've never thought of wearing my hair this way.

What do you mean *your* hair? That's not your hair. It looks like a pelt from a small animal.

Luke says everyone out here wears hairpieces, men and women both. And did you know you're not supposed to wash your face with soap? It's too harsh. Luke gave me a gentle cleanser to use instead. Oh, and I'm going to start doing pushups and crunches every morning. Luke says with a little effort, I can get my waistline back.

Who *are* you?

Ha! It's still me, Olive. I know it might seem silly, but it's been a long time since I took an interest in my appearance. And Luke's right. Little things make a big difference, don't you think?

Yes. Like picking up people at the airport who are waiting for you.

I'm sorry, Olive. As I mentioned, I just got your letter. Seymour and I were with Luke Ahtmee all day.

Yes, you told me. Now tell me where Seymour is. Maybe he'll help me find my luggage.

He's in room 402. Please don't be mad at me, Olive.

Good night, Iggy. Enjoy your new skin cleanser.

Le Beverly Hills Hotel
444 N. Rexford Drive
Beverly Hills, CA 90210

March 13

Dear Olive,

How do you like my new stationery? Isn't it cool? Phillip D. Rubbish gave it to me. He's the director of <u>Evilo Must Go!</u> Looks like I'm not going to be in the movie. (Rats.) Phillip said focus groups liked the character of Sylvester better than me. (Double rats.) So they're going to audition a bunch of boys until they find the right Sylvester.

But here's the good news: Phillip says I can be president of the Sylvester Hope Fan Club. I can't wait till you get here so I can tell you more abou

Hello, dear.

Olive! You're here!

Barely.

Isn't this the coolest hotel ever? Have you seen the swim-ming pool? It's shaped like a star. Olive, I think we should put in a pool at Spence Mansion.

Really? How interesting.

Oh, and look. Phillip gave me a cell phone! I've always wanted one. Olive? Are you okay?

Just tired, dear. You haven't seen my traveling bags, have you?

No. What do they look like?

Every piece of my luggage is adorned with the letter "O."

Sorry, Olive. I don't know where your bags could be. Unless . . . I have an idea. Stay here. I'll be right back.

March 13

Phillip D. Rubbish
Director, Buster Boy Entertainment
630 West 5th Street
Los Angeles, CA 90071

Delivered by Courier

Dear Phillip,

Thank you for sending the limo to pick me up at the air-port. It was wonderful to see my fans. They've always been so kind, but lately I've sensed the vultures circling. Everyone's hoping to get the last picture of me alive. Ah, well. That photo will fetch a pretty penny someday, I suppose. I just hope I don't kick off before we make this movie.

Moe said that you requested me specifically for this role. I'm surprised someone your age even remembers an old bird like me. But I'm eager to play the role of a ghost. I finished reading *43 Old Cemetery Road* this morning and enjoyed it immensely. I plan to start reading the script soon. Maybe tomorrow. Good-night, Phillip.

Oh, look at me! I almost forgot why I picked up this pen. I wanted to tell you that I just met the real Seymour Hope. Such a delightful young boy. He came to my door a few minutes ago to ask if I had Olive's luggage. He spoke so convincingly about his friend Olive, he almost made me believe in the "ghost of Spence Mansion."

Have you considered asking Seymour to play himself in the film? I think that boy would light up the screen with his adorable smile.

Something to think about.

Kisses,

Ivana Oscar

Ivana Oscar

P.S. One other thing, Phillip: I don't hear well and I'm too vain to wear a hearing aid. If you need to tell me anything, kindly put it in a note and slip it under my door. I'm in the penthouse suite.

PHILLIP D. RUBBISH
DIRECTOR

BUSTER BOY ENTERTAINMENT
630 WEST 5TH STREET   LOS ANGELES, CA 90071

March 14

Ivana Oscar
c/o Le Beverly Hills Hotel
444 N. Rexford Drive
Beverly Hills, CA 90210

HAND-DELIVERED

Dear Miss Oscar,

Glad you arrived safe and sound! I would've
met you at the airport myself, but I'm busy
getting ready for auditions.

I met Seymour earlier today and couldn't
agree with you more. He's a great kid.
GREAT KID! Love him to death. But he's all
wrong for the part of Sylvester.

Don't worry. I expect hundreds of experienced child actors will be lined up for the
casting call. We're holding auditions right
here in the hotel. If you want to watch,
come to the Casablanca Room on Monday at
ten o'clock.

On second thought, scratch that. You'll
just get mobbed by fans, and we certainly

don't want anything bad to happen to you
before we start filming! So just stay in
your room, relax, read the script, memorize
your lines, order room service. Everything's
on us, remember. It's in your contract.

I'll close with the words of Moe Block
Busters: Reach for the stars! Oh, wait. You
ARE A STAR! Ha ha!

Your devoted director,

Phillip D. Rubbish

Phillip D. Rubbish

P.S. I'm checking into the hotel tomorrow.
I'll be staying there while *Evilo Must Go!*
is in production.

P.P.S. The kid's almost got you believing
in the "ghost of Spence Mansion"? That's a
good one, Miss Oscar. A GOOD ONE!

From the Penthouse Suite

March 15

Seymour Hope
Le Beverly Hills Hotel, Room 402
444 N. Rexford Drive
Beverly Hills, CA 90210

Dear Seymour,

Tomorrow morning I want you to wash that goop out of your hair and let it dry outside in the sun. Don't comb it or put any products in it. Wear an Oxford cloth shirt and jeans. Go downstairs to the Casablanca Room at ten o'clock and say your name is ... Oh, I don't know. You'll think of something. Just don't use your real name for the audition. We want Phillip to think you're an experienced actor.

You're a darling boy and I'd love to work with you if I have the strength to do this film. I'm afraid I'm older than dirt.

Kisses,

Ivana Oscar

Ivana Oscar

P.S. Remember those suitcases you asked about? They must be props for the movie. I peeked inside one bag and saw the most exquisite velvet gown. I can't wait to try it on.

Le Beverly Hills Hotel
444 N. Rexford Drive
Beverly Hills, CA 90210

March 15

Dear Miss Oscar,

That's a great idea! I'm going to audition for the part.

Older than dirt? That's funny. I'll have to tell Olive that one. She's even older than you, but she always says that as long as she's laughing, she feels like a kid.

Have you met Olive yet? Those are definitely her suitcases. You might want to ask her before you try on her clothes. Olive's really great, but sometimes she has a bad temper.

—Seymour

P.S. I'll let you know how the audition goes!

Seymour Hope
Le Beverly Hills Hotel
444 N. Rexford Drive
Beverly Hills, CA 90210

BIG NEWS INSIDE
(You won't believe it!)

Photos enclosed. Please don't bend!

HOLLYWOOD

The Ghastly Times
20 Scary Street
Ghastly, Illinois

Los Angeles
CA
PM
MAR 17

USA
72¢

➤THE GHASTLY TIMES◄

Friday, March 20
Cliff Hanger, Editor

"We're Living in Ghastly Times"

50 cents
Morning Edition

The Kid Stays in the Picture!

Seymour Hope will have a major role in a movie based on his family's book, *43 Old Cemetery Road.*

"It's kind of confusing," said Hope in a letter sent to this newspaper. "The movie is supposedly based on our book, but it's completely different. It will even have a different title, *Evilo Must Go!*"

According to Hope, Ivana Oscar encouraged him to audition for the role of the boy who lives in Spence Mansion—in other words, himself—though the character in the movie will be called Sylvester.

"I didn't think I'd get the part," Hope said in his letter. "When I met the director, he told me he wanted an experienced actor to play the role. But I figured I had nothing to lose by auditioning. It was fun and easy to pretend to be me. The only hard part was lying about my name. I couldn't use my real name, so I called myself Willie Shadow instead. It's the name of my dog and my cat."

After selecting Seymour for the role, director Phillip D. Rubbish told Hope to continue using the stage name Willie Shadow. "Phillip says it has real star power," Hope wrote.

As for the rest of his family, Hope reported that his father is adjusting to his new teeth. (See side story.) And what about his mother?

"Olive is spending a lot of time in Miss Oscar's room," Hope said. "At first Miss Oscar didn't believe Olive was real, but I think she's getting the idea now. She saw clothes floating from Olive's suitcases to the closet. I had to explain that it was Olive unpacking."

Hope says the audition was fun and easy.

The only disappointment so far, said Hope, was discovering that Olive won't be in the movie. "Phillip says Evilo is a stronger character than Olive," wrote Hope. "Obviously he hasn't met Olive yet."

Grumply's New Smile Says It All

A new wardrobe and hairstyle. A thousand-watt smile. And a small part in a big movie.

Ignatius B. Grumply has a new look—and a new outlook to go with it. According to Seymour Hope's letter, Grumply was asked to play himself in the movie.

"The director told Iggy that the role of Ignatius B. Grumply was kind of a nothing

Continued on page 2, column 1

SMILE *Continued from page 1, column 2*

part," Hope said. "That was pretty rude, if you ask me, but I don't think Iggy was upset by it. Ever since he got his makeover, a lot of ladies have been following him, asking for his autograph. He's enjoying the attention."

Grumply shows off his new look.

What Was *That?*

The Federal Aviation Administration (FAA) has launched an investigation after receiving reports of odd phenomena on a recent flight from Ghastly to Los Angeles.

"Several passengers reported seeing a pair of opera glasses floating through the first-class cabin," said FAA spokesman Don Worrie. "Other passengers heard what sounded like someone stomping angrily up and down the aisle."

Anyone with information relating to last Friday's flight is urged to contact the FAA.

Freaky Faucet Floods Spence Mansion

Even when he's knee-deep in trouble, Briss refuses help or advice from Balm.

Hugh Briss spent yesterday fixing a leaky faucet in a third-floor bathroom in Spence Mansion. Or so he thought.

When he returned from lunch, he found a river of water flowing down the front steps of the house. "It looked like a scene out of the movie *Titanic*," said Briss.

Librarian M. Balm offered to help clean up the mess. He also offered to lend Briss a copy of *43 Old Cemetery Road*. "I thought it might be useful for Mr. Briss to know about Spence Mansion and the people who live there," said Balm.

But Balm was dissed by Briss, who said he had no need of books.

"Everything I need to know is right up here," Briss said, tapping his head.

Page 3 **The Ghastly Times** March 20

SPECIAL ADVERTISING SUPPLEMENT

Coming Soon to a Theater Near You . . .

Evilo Must Go!

Starring
Ivana Oscar
as Evilo
in her final film appearance *ever*
Introducing
Willie Shadow
as Sylvester
with
Ignatius B. Grumply
as himself

Written and Directed by
Phillip D. Rubbish
A Buster Boy Entertainment Production

Rated R

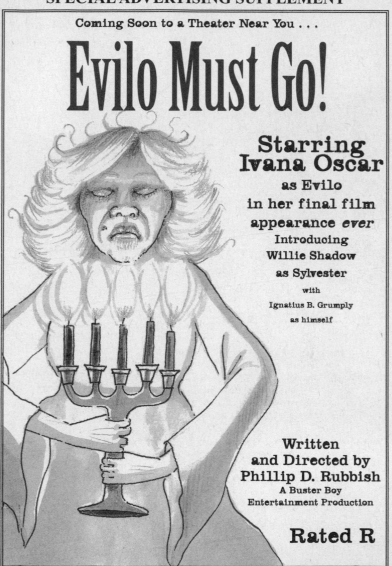

March 20

Phillip D. Rubbish
c/o Le Beverly Hills Hotel
444 N. Rexford Drive
Beverly Hills, CA 90210

Dear Mr. Rubbish,

I don't know where to begin. With the fact that no one sent a limousine to meet me at the airport? Or the fact that I'm sleeping in Ivana Oscar's bathtub because there are no available rooms in this hotel? (And don't you dare suggest I bunk with Ignatius or Seymour. They need their privacy as much as I do.)

Or how about the fact that I, Olive C. Spence, have no role in this movie? Do you not realize, Mr. Rubbish, that 43 Old Cemetery Road is the address of *my* mansion? Are you not aware that *I* am the one who came up with the idea of writing the book *43 Old Cemetery Road* in the first place?

Maybe not. Maybe you really are as foolish as you seem, in which case I will simply and politely request that you rewrite the script *immediately* so that *I* am the star of this film. With the proper amount of coaxing, I might be willing to play myself in such a movie.

Yours in spirit,

Olive C. Spence
A real femme fatale

PHILLIP D. RUBBISH
DIRECTOR
BUSTER BOY ENTERTAINMENT
630 WEST 5TH STREET   LOS ANGELES, CA 90071

<u>Temporary Address</u>
Le Beverly Hills Hotel
Room 322

March 21

Seymour Hope
Le Beverly Hills Hotel, Room 402
444 N. Rexford Drive
Beverly Hills, CA 90210

Dear Seymour,

Ha ha, kid! I don't know who told you that
pranks and practical jokes are common on
every film set. But seriously, kiddo, we've
got a lot of work ahead of us. A LOT OF
WORK! You in particular have a lot of lines
to memorize.

So lay off the goofy "ghost" notes slipped
under the hotel door, okay?

Thanks,

Phillip D. Rubbish

Phillip D. Rubbish

The Sylvester Hope Fan Club
Seymour Hope, President

Le Beverly Hills Hotel
444 N. Rexford Drive
Beverly Hills, CA 90210

Hand—Delivered

March 21

Dear Mr. Rubbish,

I haven't written any notes to you until now. It was probably Olive. That's the only way she can communicate.

Hey, should I wear my sunglasses in the movie? A girl just told me I look really cute in them. Let me know what you think. Thanks!

—Seymour

P.S. Also, should I tell my fans I'm Sylvester or Willie Shadow or just plain Seymour? I'm kind of confused about that.

Le Beverly Hills Hotel

"Where the Stars Stay in Style"
444 N. Rexford Drive
Beverly Hills, CA 90210

March 21

Dear Mr. Rubbish,

Here's another thing: You are turning my son into a monster. He now spends hours each day preening like a rooster in front of the mirror. I realize this is typical for an eleven-year-old boy. I've read all the parenting books in my local library, so I know it's perfectly natural for a child his age to try on various styles and personalities.

But now you've got Seymour playing a boy named Willie Shadow who's playing a boy named Sylvester who's playing Seymour. You're going to drive the poor child mad! You're also turning Ignatius into a parody of himself, but he's old enough to know better.

I strongly suggest you rewrite this story *immediately* or you will be sorry.

Sincerely angry,

Olive C. Spence
A real femme fatale

P.S. I also suggest you change the R rating to G so children my son's age can see this movie.

PHILLIP D. RUBBISH
DIRECTOR
BUSTER BOY ENTERTAINMENT
630 WEST 5TH STREET   LOS ANGELES, CA 90071

<u>Temporary Address</u>
Le Beverly Hills Hotel
Room 322

March 21

Myra Manes
Personal Adviser & Assistant
    to Moe Block Busters
Buster Boy Entertainment
630 West 5th Street
Los Angeles, CA 90071

Dear Myra,

This is a long shot, but you're not by
any chance slipping jokey funny ha-ha
scary letters under my door, are you?
Someone's pretending to be Olive C.
Spence, and I'm wondering if it's you.

Phillip D. Rubbish

Phillip D. Rubbish

MYRA MANES

PERSONAL ADVISER & ASSISTANT TO MOE BLOCK BUSTERS

BUSTER BOY ENTERTAINMENT

630 WEST 5TH STREET   LOS ANGELES, CA 90071

March 23

Phillip D. Rubbish
Le Beverly Hills Hotel, Room 322
444 N. Rexford Drive
Beverly Hills, CA 90210

Dear Phillip,

No, it's not me. But I'm glad you wrote. I want to discuss something with you.

I've seen the billboards around town for *Evilo Must Go!* Are you sure you want to advertise that this will be Miss Oscar's final film appearance? Of course, it's true. I included a death clause in Miss Oscar's contract that obligates her to die while making this film.

But may I suggest you wait until *after* she dies before you use her death in the marketing campaign? We don't want anyone to blame the studio for Miss Oscar's demise.

Just trying to be helpful.

Myra Manes

Myra Manes

PHILLIP D. RUBBISH
DIRECTOR
BUSTER BOY ENTERTAINMENT
630 WEST 5TH STREET   LOS ANGELES, CA 90071

March 24

Myra Manes
Personal Adviser & Assistant
  to Moe Block Busters
Buster Boy Entertainment
630 West 5th Street
Los Angeles, CA 90071

Dear Myra,

You're absolutely right! I'm going to
remove all references to Miss Oscar's
death pronto. PRONTO!

Thanks, Myra. You sure are one clever
cookie. By the way, I fully understand
the death clause. After all, it was *my*
idea.

Phillip D. Rubbish

Phillip D. Rubbish

P.S. Please destroy this letter after
you read it. Better safe than sorry, if
you know what I mean. SAFE is better
than SORRY!

MYRA MANES

PERSONAL ADVISER & ASSISTANT TO MOE BLOCK BUSTERS

BUSTER BOY ENTERTAINMENT

630 WEST 5TH STREET   LOS ANGELES, CA 90071

March 25

Phillip D. Rubbish
Le Beverly Hills Hotel, Room 322
444 N. Rexford Drive
Beverly Hills, CA 90210

Dear Phillip,

I never destroy documents. And for the record, the death clause[*]
was *my* idea. I predict it will go down in history as the finest sen-
tence ever written in Hollywood.

Perhaps I'm tougher than you think.

Helpfully yours,

Myra Manes

Myra Manes

[*]The undersigned hereby agrees to die of natural causes or otherwise while
making the film to guarantee box-office success and cult status for the movie.

March 26

My, my, Mr. Rubbish.

What an interesting letter from Myra Manes.
Now I'm beginning to understand why you didn't
cast me to star in your movie. How could I pos-
sibly comply with the death clause when I'm
already dead?

This is beginning to feel less like a Hollywood
blockbuster and more like a Shakespearean
tragedy. Mr. Shakespeare loved a good story
about power and hubris. You know what hubris
is, don't you, Phillip? Excessive pride and ar-
rogance. Hubris is often found in great literary
characters, but it exists in real life as well. In
fact, hubris was considered a crime in ancient
Greece.

Don't worry. I have no plans to sue you. But I
would like a starring role in this drama.

Your favorite femme fatale,

Olive C. Spence

PHILLIP D. RUBBISH
DIRECTOR
BUSTER BOY ENTERTAINMENT
630 WEST 5TH STREET   LOS ANGELES, CA 90071

<u>Temporary Address</u>
Le Beverly Hills Hotel
Room 322

March 26

INTERNATIONAL EXPRESS MAIL

Moe Block Busters
Buster Boy Retreat
MBB's Private Island
Somewhere in the Caribbean

Dear Mr. Busters,

I know I'm not supposed to bother you
when you're on vacation, but I was just
wondering: Do you think it was bad luck
to add that clause in Miss Oscar's contract? You know, the clause *I* invented
that requires her to die while we're
making this movie?

Miss Oscar hasn't mentioned it yet. I
don't think she's read a single page of
her contract. But I've been thinking.

What if it sorta, y'know, *curses* the movie?

I know, I know. You're probably thinking: "Snap out of it, Phillip! It's just the jitters. Every new studio boss gets 'em." But I'm telling you, the strangest things have been happening.

Stop stalling, Rubbish. Tell Mr. Busters there's a ghost in your hotel room who wants to be in this movie.

See? This is what I'm talking about. This bad special-effects stuff. It's like something out of an amateur ghost movie.

Are you calling me an amateur? Do you want me to tickle you so hard you wet your pants?

See? There it is again. It's nothing we could even use in the film. It's too corny and G-rated for our demo, but . . . Oh! Ha! Ha! HA! Stop! STOP!

I'll stop tickling when you give me a part in the movie.

What? No! STOP. Ha! HA! Boss, do you see what I'm talking about here? Ha ha HA! Help me!!!!

There's no help for you, Rubbish.

Ha! This is kinda freaking me out a little! What should I DO?

Phillip

Phillip D. Rubbish

P.S. Myra Manes is being mean to me. I'm going to fire her, if you don't mind.

Oh, for pity's sake!

March 27

INTERNATIONAL EXPRESS MAIL

Phillip D. Rubbish
Le Beverly Hills Hotel, Room 322
444 N. Rexford Drive
Beverly Hills, CA 90210 USA

Dear Phillip,

Are you *kidding* me?

I get you the hottest book in America. I bring in the folksy
Grampa Grumply and that Sebastian kid. I get Myra to
draw up a contract that guarantees Ivana Oscar will die
while making this movie. (By the by, the death clause was
my idea, not yours.) And now you're sending me letters
written in—*what?*—magic ghost ink? What are you, Rubbish? Ten years old?

Okay, so I didn't give you a big budget for this film. Get over
it! Because I'll tell you right now, audiences are NOT going
to be satisfied with dime-store special effects like the one
you used in that letter.

Just make me a low-budget blockbuster with some snazzy
(but cheap) special effects, will you? It's not that hard. *Evilo*

Must Go! is basically *Return of the Sharks* meets *Explosions 2,* with a ghost named Evilo substituting for the shark and the explosions. Noodle around in the prop room and dig out some fake blood, vomit, and werewolf claws. You can't go wrong with those.

I don't want to hear another word from you until my plane lands in Los Angeles on April 10. I arrive just before midnight. Have Myra send a limo. (And *no,* you can't fire her!)

Reaching for my beach towel,

Moe Block Busters

Moe Block Busters

P.S. I just looked at the production schedule. You're supposed to begin shooting tomorrow. Stop writing goofy letters and start making a movie already, will you? And keep an eye on the bottom line. I don't want this film to go one *penny* over budget.

THE HOLLYWOOD WHISPER

Sunday, March 29   "Movie News and Secrets You're Just *Dying* to Hear" $1.50

Fans Mob *Evilo* Set

"We want Willie Shadow! We want Willie Shadow! We want Willie Shadow!"

That chant repeated yesterday by an estimated ten thousand young fans prevented Phillip D. Rubbish from starting production of *Evilo Must Go!*

Some Hollywood insiders seemed surprised by how quickly Willie Shadow has catapulted to stardom. "They haven't even made the film yet, and already the kid has fans," said film critic Matt N. Nay. "Well, that's Hollywood for you."

Willie Shadow, who will play the role of Sylvester in *Evilo Must Go!*, made only a brief comment to fans.

Willie Shadow is mobbed by his adoring fans.

"I wish my dog and cat could see me now," said the young actor, whose shy demeanor and love of animals will only add to his star appeal.

Ivana Wants a New Script

Oscar says Rubbish ruined a good ghost story.

Ivana Oscar, known to fans as Hollywood's favorite femme fatale, says she's unhappy with the script for *Evilo Must Go!*

"The screenplay bears no resemblance to the book *43 Old Cemetery Road*," said Oscar. "There's not even a mention of Olive, the ghost who lives in Spence Mansion. I happen to find Olive completely believable, unlike the ridiculous caricature of a ghost called Evilo in this script. I plan to talk to Phillip about it. Or rather, I'll write him a letter."

It might be a waste of time and ink.

"The script is perfect as is," said director and screenplay writer Phillip D. Rubbish. "Besides, there's no money in the budget for a rewrite or any new characters. Do you hear me out there? Read my lips: No. New. Characters!"

Tooth or Dare

Before Ignatius B. Grumply can play himself in *Evilo Must Go!* he must pay another visit to Dr. Miles Smyle. Two weeks after having his natural teeth covered with porcelain veneers, Grumply has developed an unfortunate lisp.

"I'm fairly thertain thith wath cauthed by my rethent dental protheedure," said Grumply. "In any cathe, I'm going to get thith fixthed thoon. It'th embarrathing."

Phillip D. Rubbish said Buster Boy Entertainment will cover the cost.

"We can't begin shooting without Mr. Grumply," said Rubbish.

Grumply, author of *43 Old Cemetery Road*, recently transferred all rights in the book and characters, including what has been written and what will be written, to Buster Boy Entertainment. A source close to the project says Grumply was paid nothing in the deal.

Grumply's new teeth are causing an unfortunate lisp.

Feds Continue to Gather Information

Officials with the Federal Aviation Administration (FAA) are continuing their investigation of a flight earlier this month from Ghastly, Illinois, to Los Angeles.

"One passenger reported seeing a floating feather boa," said FAA spokesman Don Worrie. "We have referred that passenger to a mental health facility."

Anyone with information about the flight from Ghastly to Los Angeles on Friday, March 13, is urged to contact the FAA. "But folks, please, only credible information is helpful," said Worrie. "No more kooky Friday the thirteenth stuff, please."

Le Beverly Hills Hotel

"Where the Stars Stay in Style"
444 N. Rexford Drive
Beverly Hills, CA 90210

March 30

Phillip D. Rubbish
Le Beverly Hills Hotel, Room 322
444 N. Rexford Drive
Beverly Hills, CA 90210

Dear Phillip,

Thanks for making the appointment with Dr. Smyle. I'm sure he'll be able to fix my lisp. Until then I'll stay in my room and practice my lines. I'm really excited to shoot the scene where I

Which scene are you really excited to shoot, Iggy?

Olive! Would it be so hard for you to knock on a door rather than slinking into my room and lurking over my shoulder?

I'll learn to knock if you'll admit this movie is a complete disaster.

Well, I'll admit I *thought* it was going to be a disaster. But dental appointments aside, this is the most fun I've had in years.

Oh, really? And does it bother you at all that I have no part in the film? Not even a cameo role?

Of *course* it bothers me, Olive. That's why I've talked at length with Phillip about this. He feels strongly that audiences are tired of what he calls "little old lady ghosts." What audiences want today is a nasty ghost named Evilo. You have to admit that's pretty good.

I will admit no such thing! What about the fact that Buster Boy Entertainment claims it now owns everything we've ever written or will write? Or that Moe Block Busters didn't pay us a thin *dime?*

I know, I know. The contract was unfortunate, but surely there's some wiggle room there. I wonder how the *Hollywood Whisper* found out we weren't paid anything.

You wonder, do you? Well, I'll tell you. I slipped a note to a reporter, informing him of this terrible outrage.

Ugh. Phillip's not going to like that.

Do you think I care what Phillip D. Rubbish likes or doesn't like? Iggy, this film is a tragedy in the making. Mark my words, someone's going to get hurt. We have to nullify that hideous contract. Please tell me you agree with me on that much.

I do, Olive. But can we talk about this later? I have an appointment with Dr. Smyle in the morning. Phillip says if my teeth were a bit longer, it would give me a more youthful smile. I don't know. I need to exfoliate and then decide.

Do as you please! I'll get Seymour to help me.

Le Beverly Hills Hotel
444 N. Rexford Drive
Beverly Hills, CA 90210

March 30

A Letter to Fans:

In response to popular demand, Willie Shadow will make him-self available for a meet-and-greet photo session tomorrow by the pool of Le Beverly Hills Hotel. Bring your cameras and autograph pens for an afterno

Seymour! What on earth are you doing?

Hey, Olive! I didn't hear you come in. I'm writing a letter to my fans. How are you?

Furious.

Why?

Because of this monstrous movie deal. I cannot tell you how much I dislike that vile little Rub-bish man.

Olive, I think if you got to know Phillip better, you'd really like him. He has a ton of good ideas. In fact, I just thought of something. Do you want me to talk to Phillip about making you the president of the Evilo fan club?

Have you lost your mind, Seymour? No, I do not want to be the president of someone *else's* fan club. That does it.

What?

It's the last straw. I'm finished with Mr. Busters and his bevy of blockheads. I want you and Iggy to come to your senses and return home with me so we can get back to work on our book. Have you forgotten that we've promised readers new chapters by April 13?

I know. But can we just stay here long enough to make the movie? Phillip says once we get started, it will go really fast. And Phillip says

Phillip says this and Phillip says that. If Phillip told you to go jump in a lake, would you?

I wouldn't, but Sylvester might. I have to start thinking like the character I'm playing. I have to get into my
character's head and try to think his thoughts. If
Sylvester thought he should go jump in a lake, I guess
I'd have to do it—unless Willie Shadow thought Sylvester
wouldn't do that. I know it sounds complicated, but Phillip
says acting is all about artistic integrity.

Integrity? What does Phillip D. Rubbish know
about integrity? I cannot listen to another word
of this nonsense. Good-bye.

Olive, where are you going?

Home!

≋ Ivana Oscar ≋

Screen Legend, Stage Icon, Winner of (Almost) Every Award Under the Sun

From the Penthouse Suite

March 30

Dear Phillip,

You should be ashamed of yourself. To think I agreed to play
a part in a movie that bears no resemblance to the book is one
thing. But then to learn that this story was essentially stolen
from its creators, well, that tops everything. If I weren't such an
old woman, I'd have a mind to

Thank you for understanding, dear.

Something's wrong with my eyes. I'm seeing things. I wonder if I
am dying.

You look perfectly fine to me.

What in the world? Who are you? A reporter? A fan? Don't tell
me you're a stalker. I'll call the police.

No need. It's only me, Olive C. Spence.

The ghost of Spence Mansion?

That's right.

Do you mean to tell me you're really Olive C. Spence?

One and the same. I've been sleeping in your bathtub. There are no available rooms in this hotel.

I thought I heard noises in the bathroom.

I apologize. I tend to snore when I'm upset. But don't worry. I'm leaving tomorrow.

This is fascinating. Am I able to communicate with you because I'm so near death myself?

Maybe. But as I noted earlier, you look fine to me. The picture of health, in fact.

Very kind of you to say, Miss Spence.

Please, call me Olive.

Then you must call me Ivana. It's nice to make a new friend.

We're allies, dear. I'm as fed up with Phillip D. Rubbish as you are. He and Moe Block Busters are scoundrels.

Yes, and smart scoundrels, too. That deal they cooked up is awful. With one stroke of the pen, Ignatius signed away everything your family has worked so hard to create. He must feel terrible.

I wish. Iggy's too busy admiring his new reflection in the mirror.

Oh, that often happens in this city. What about Sylvester?

If you mean Seymour, the boy's brain has stopped working. He's more concerned about posing for pictures than drawing pictures.

And the worst part is, everything he draws or you write now belongs to Buster Boy Entertainment.

As if those fools even respected my work. They find my character too quiet and old-ladylike. It's maddening, I tell you, absolutely maddening! But Ivana, I shouldn't complain. Your contract is even worse than ours.

What do you mean?

Didn't you read the contract you signed with Buster Boy Entertainment?

Heavens, no. Those movie contracts are so dull.

Then you don't know about the death clause?

The what?

Oh, dear. I hate to tell you this, but it's right there on page 547 of your contract. I read the whole thing yesterday. The death clause says this: *The undersigned*—that would be you—*hereby agrees to die of natural causes or otherwise while making the film to guarantee box-office success and cult status for the movie.*

I don't know what to say. I . . . I . . .

Ivana, are you laughing or crying?

Both! I mean, honestly, have you ever heard of anything more ridiculous in your life?

No. Not in my death, either.

They're demanding that I die of natural causes . . . or otherwise? I don't understand.

I think it means if you don't die on your own, they'll kill you. I'm sorry, Ivana. Are you all right?

Yes, I'm fine, actually. I'm just chuckling at the absurdity of it all. And that makes me feel more alive. Is there a connection?

Between laughter and life? Of course. Laughter has always been my best beauty secret. Do you want to hear something that will *really* make you laugh?

Tell me.

I thought I was coming to Hollywood to become a movie star. Ha! I thought when Moe Block Busters said he had the perfect femme fatale for this movie, he was talking about *me!* Ha ha ha! After all, I am a deadly woman. Oh, Ivana, it's so funny when you think about it. I could die again laughing.

You were dying to become a movie star, and the movie makers are *dying* to kill me. Ha ha ha!

HA HA HA!

HA HA HA HA HA!

HA HA HA!

HA HA HA HA HA!

HA! HA! HA! HA! HA!

Oh, Olive, what if . . . Maybe it's crazy. I'm almost embarrassed to write it.

Whisper it in my ear, dear.

There, I said it. Did you hear me? You're not answering and I feel a strange breeze.

I'm sorry, Ivana. That was me laughing again.

Really? Does that mean you like my idea?

Like it? I love it. There's nothing on earth scarier to a man like Phillip D. Rubbish than an old broad who refuses to act her age. Now I almost wish I weren't going home tomorrow.

Olive, please stay. I need your help to pull this off.

I'm tempted.

Really. I can't do this alone. I need a good writer, a hairdresser, and a makeup artist.

Oh, no. You look perfect just the way you are.

Do you think so?

Absolutely.

But what should I say? What are my lines?

Scoot over, Ivana. I shall write the perfect script for you.

THE DAILY SCANDAL

Tuesday, March 31 "Hot Rumors Served Fresh, Day and Night!" **$1.00**

Max Schlock, Editor Evening Edition

Ivana SMOOCH! Screen Legend Says "I Love Rubbish!"

Ivana Oscar was spotted this morning on the set of *Evilo Must Go!* planting a great big smoocharoo on the cheek of director Phillip D. Rubbish.

"Being in a new relationship makes me feel so alive," cooed Oscar, 92.

Scandal reporters have learned that Rubbish specifically requested Oscar for the role of Evilo. Rubbish has also been seen slipping secret love notes under Miss Oscar's hotel room door.

"Sure, their backgrounds might seem different at first," said makeup artist Sarah Mirror. "But they have a lot in common when you think about it. I can see Phillip and Ivana chatting endlessly in front of a romantic fire about their favorite movies."

"Ivana is exactly the kind of woman Phillip loves," added film critic Matt N. Nay. "She's smart, sophisticated, and, of course, extremely mature."

Rubbish, 42, refused to comment on his new relationship with the elderly actress.

Oscar was less shy about her feelings.

"I love Rubbish," she told reporters. Then she kicked up her heels and said it again louder. "I want to tell the world that I really, really love Rubbish!"

Fans Feel Cheated by Mr. Conceited
Only Willie Shadow Knows Why He's Such a Big-Headed Brat

Memo to young heartthrob: Lose the sunglasses and the cooler-than-thou attitude.

That was the takeaway message from this afternoon's meet-and-greet session at Le Beverly Hills Hotel. Willie Shadow, who will play Sylvester in the upcoming film *Evilo Must Go!,* had promised fans a chance to have their picture taken with him. But the pre-teen idol refused to remove his sunglasses or answer any personal questions.

"I just wanted to know more about his pets," said Mary Mee. "But Willie Shadow wouldn't answer me. He was just plain rude!"

Male fans were equally disappointed.

"I asked Willie where he was from," said Holden Hands. "But he refused to say anything. Consider me a former fan."

Little is known about Willie Shadow other than the fact that he was chosen to play the part of Sylvester from more than

Willie Shadow ignores fans.

500 young actors who auditioned for the role. You can bet reporters are digging into his past even as you read these words.

Fangs a Lot!
Grumply Not Happy with Tooth or Consequences

Grumply is grumpy about his new teeth.

Ignatius B. Grumply got a new set of choppers this morning. And what a set!

"I thpethifically told Dr. Mileth Thmyle that I wanted a thet of teeth that would make me theem like I wath in my early fortieth rather than my thixtieth. And thith ith what he giveth me? Pleathe!"

"Relax, this is Hollywood," Smyle said. "Bigger is better. I like my smiles to be a mile wide. But if Mr. Grumply wants me to file them down a bit, sure, I can do that."

Grumply has another appointment with Dr. Smyle scheduled for next week.

"Thank heaventh Buthter Boy Entertainment ith paying for all thith," said Grumply. "It'th exthpenthive."

MEMO FROM THE DIRECTOR

TO: Cast and crew of *Evilo Must Go!*
FR: Phillip D. Rubbish
RE: Can we use some discretion, please?
PLEASE?
DATE: March 31

Our hotel is surrounded by paparazzi and
tabloid reporters. They make their money
by taking unflattering photos and writing
shocking stories about celebrities. They're
not above making up ridiculous stuff. I
mean seriously, RIDICULOUS STUFF! A little
discretion would be appreciated.

From the Penthouse Suite

March 31

Dear Phillip,

I'm sorry if you were taken by surprise by my interview with the *Daily Scandal*. I meant every word of it. And the kiss? Well, what can I say? I meant that, too.

Would you like to pop over to my room later tonight? I'm having a little party. I know you're busy, so if you can't make it, I'll understand. I hope the music doesn't bother you, dear. Because of my poor hearing, I need to really crank it up.

Kisses!

Ivana

Le Beverly Hills Hotel

"Where the Stars Stay in Style"
444 N. Rexford Drive
Beverly Hills, CA 90210

Bill Moore
Hotel Manager

April 1

Dear Mr. Rubbish,

Due to the number of complaints we received last night about loud music and laughter from the penthouse suite, we are adding a service charge of $7,500 to that room.

The charge will appear on Buster Boy Entertainment's bill along with the boogie board rentals and catering fees charged by Miss Oscar for her party tomorrow.

Bill Moore

Bill Moore

P.S. No, this is not an April Fool's joke.

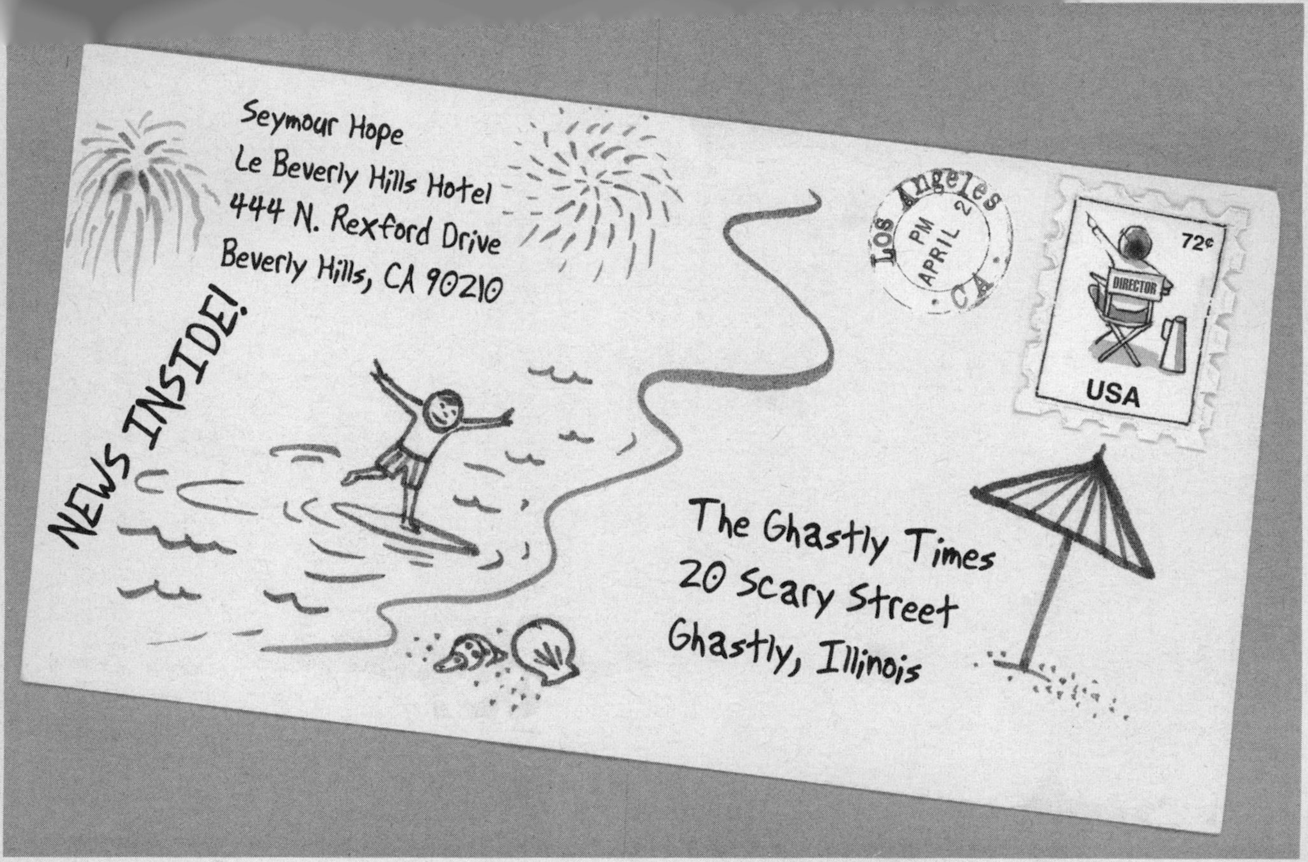
Seymour Hope
Le Beverly Hills Hotel
444 N. Rexford Drive
Beverly Hills, CA 90210
NEWS INSIDE!
Los Angeles
PM
APRIL 2
CA
72¢
DIRECTOR
USA
The Ghastly Times
20 Scary Street
Ghastly, Illinois

➤THE GHASTLY TIMES◄

Sunday, April 5
Cliff Hanger, Editor

"We're Living in Ghastly Times"

$1.50
Morning Edition

Bathing Beauties, Explosions and a Werewolf on the Beach!

**Oscar hosts a beach party
for cast and crew.**

It sounds like a summer movie by Moe Block Busters. But according to Seymour Hope's recent letter and cell phone photos, it was just another day in Hollywood. Looking out his hotel window, Hope saw not only bathing beauties and fireworks displays, but also a werewolf—or at least a father who looked frightful as a result of recent dental work. (See letter below.)

**Grumply chases after his
runaway hairpiece.**

Letter from Seymour

Dear Everyone,

Hello! How are things there?

Things are okay here. Iggy doesn't like his new veneers. (Who knew teeth could be so complicated?) But Dr. Smyle says he can fix them. I wish somebody could fix the other stuff going on around here.

Olive got mad at Iggy and me the other night. She thinks Hollywood has changed us (and not in a good way), so she left. I hope she made it back to Ghastly okay. Olive, if you're reading this, I'm really sorry you don't have a part in this movie. I'm beginning to wish I didn't, either.

Continued on page 2

LETTER *Continued from page 1*

Being a movie star is not all it's cracked up to be. I made a lot of people mad the other day at a photo op. Everyone thinks I'm Willie Shadow, but as you know, there is no Willie Shadow, other than my dog and cat. I just made up that name for my audition. I'm trying to be an actor, but I'm not sure if I should be playing Sylvester, Willie Shadow, or just me. It's confusing.

I couldn't even go to the beach party today because of all the paparazzi. Phillip D. Rubbish, the director, told me he didn't want any more negative stories about me in the tabloids.

So I'm watching the party from my hotel window. You should see Ivana Oscar on a boogie board. Uh-oh. Iggy's hairpiece just blew off his head. He's running after it down the beach.

Well, I better get back to memorizing my lines. It's sort of like memorizing multiplication tables—boring but necessary.

Here's one good thing I can report: I haven't talked to Iggy about this yet, but I am definitely going to see *Evilo Must Go!* when it comes out in theaters. I don't care what it's rated. My parents have to let me see it after all the work I've put into it.

I'll write again soon. Take care, and please tell Willie, Shadow, and the kittens that I miss them. Olive, if you're reading this, I hope you know that I miss you most of all.

—Seymour

P.S. Iggy caught his hairpiece.

Holy Moley!

Briss battles moles outside Spence Mansion.

Well, it seemed like a good idea.

Hugh Briss thought he could get rid of a few moles at Spence Mansion by filling the mole holes with a smelly gel called Holy Moley.

"I ordered the stuff online," said Briss. "It's one hundred percent natural and really cheap."

It was also really effective in attracting moles, skunks, possums, raccoons and muskrats. Within hours, more than fifty rodents were picnicking comfortably in the grass surrounding Spence Mansion.

This is the second mishap that's taken place under Briss's watch.

"I tried to warn him," said M. Balm, chief librarian at the Ghastly Public Library. "But Mr. Briss has an ego the size of Spence Mansion's cupola. You can't tell him anything."

MYRA MANES

PERSONAL ADVISER & ASSISTANT TO MOE BLOCK BUSTERS

BUSTER BOY ENTERTAINMENT

630 WEST 5TH STREET   LOS ANGELES, CA 90071

DELIVERED BY COURIER

April 5

Phillip D. Rubbish
Le Beverly Hills Hotel, Room 322
444 N. Rexford Drive
Beverly Hills, CA 90210

Phillip:

A gentle reminder: According to the contract, Ivana Oscar must die while making the film. "Making the film," as defined in the contract, includes rehearsals, filming, or approved breaks if she is on the set of *Evilo Must Go!* An accident with firecrackers or a boogie board would not satisfy the terms of the contract, if that's what you were trying to achieve with the recent beach party.

If you need help enforcing the death clause, let me know.

Helpfully yours,

Myra Manes

Myra Manes

PHILLIP D. RUBBISH
DIRECTOR
BUSTER BOY ENTERTAINMENT
630 WEST 5TH STREET   LOS ANGELES, CA 90071

<u>Temporary Address</u>
Le Beverly Hills Hotel
Room 322

April 6

Myra Manes
Personal Adviser & Assistant
    to Moe Block Busters
Buster Boy Entertainment
630 West 5th Street
Los Angeles, CA 90071

Dear Myra,

The beach party was Miss Oscar's idea,
not mine.

Truth is, Myra, I don't know what to do.
When Miss Oscar arrived in Los Angeles
last month, she could barely walk. Now
she's dancing on tables and hosting
beach parties for the cast and crew.
Instead of dying, Miss Oscar seems to be
getting younger and stronger. I don't
get it. She's 92 years old. How can she
ride a boogie board?

Okay, here's what I *do* know: Ivana Oscar has to die for this lousy film to be a success.

Despicable, Rubbish. Truly despicable.

What? Ack!! Never mind that line above, Myra. I didn't write it.

Of course you didn't write it. I wrote it.

Ignore that, Myra. I've got to type faster. What I'm trying to say is that the death clause in Miss Oscar's contract gives me the right to demand that she die either by natural causes or otherwise. But . . . I can't do it, Myra. I just can't. How can I order a little old lady to die? I've tried and tried to think of a way to do it, but I can't. I JUST CAN'T!

That's the first decent thing you've said in a month. You really couldn't kill a person, could you?

Huh? No. Wait. Who am I talking to? Ha ha! Isn't this weird, Myra? Here's the thing: I don't think I could kill someone, especially not a little old lady who has a crush on me.

Good for you. But you're still rotten to the core, Rubbish.

I know I am. I really am rotten! ROTTEN! And it's served me well in the past. But now I'm in a jam, Myra. A real pickle.

I'll say.

I'm saying it! Mr. Busters is counting on me to make a blockbuster movie. But how can I? The script I wrote is garbage. Miss Oscar shows no sign of dying. Grumply's teeth are costing me a fortune. The movie is three million dollars over budget, and we haven't even started filming yet.

Myra, if you could offer me any advice or help, I would really, REALLY appreciate it.

Sincerely desperate,

Phillip

Phillip D. Rubbish

MYRA MANES

PERSONAL ADVISER & ASSISTANT TO MOE BLOCK BUSTERS

BUSTER BOY ENTERTAINMENT
630 WEST 5TH STREET   LOS ANGELES, CA 90071

HAND-DELIVERED

April 7

Phillip D. Rubbish
Le Beverly Hills Hotel, Room 322
444 N. Rexford Drive
Beverly Hills, CA 90210

Rubbish:

You Brits are always so weak and melodramatic. But never mind that. I'll help you on two conditions:

1) I become the director of *Evilo Must Go!*

2) You acknowledge that I am the sole author of the death clause.

If you agree, sign the enclosed contract.

Helpfully yours,

Myra Manes
Myra Manes

PHILLIP D. RUBBISH
DIRECTOR
BUSTER BOY ENTERTAINMENT
630 WEST 5TH STREET   LOS ANGELES, CA 90071

<u>Temporary Address</u>
Le Beverly Hills Hotel
Room 322

April 7

Myra Manes
Personal Adviser & Assistant
    to Moe Block Busters
Buster Boy Entertainment
630 West 5th Street
Los Angeles, CA 90071

Dear Myra,

Yes. Fine. Okay. OKAY! Here's the contract.

If you need me, I'll be by the pool.

Phillip

Phillip D. Rubbish

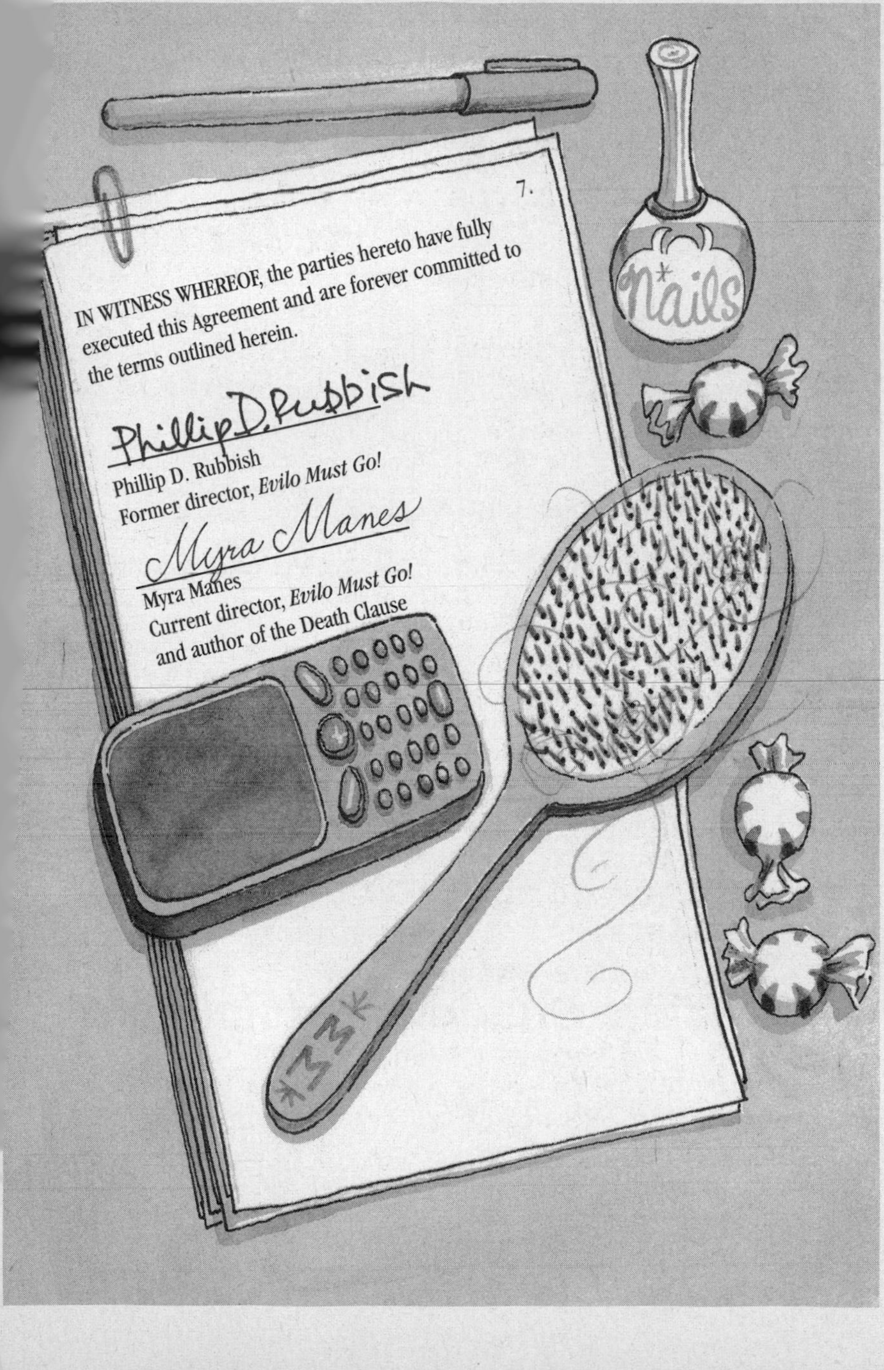
7.
IN WITNESS WHEREOF, the parties hereto have fully executed this Agreement and are forever committed to the terms outlined herein.
Phillip D. Rubbish
Phillip D. Rubbish
Former director, Evilo Must Go!
Myra Manes
Myra Manes
Current director, Evilo Must Go!
and author of the Death Clause
Nails

THE HOLLYWOOD WHISPER

Wednesday, April 8 "Movie News and Secrets You're Just *Dying* to Hear" $1.50

Have You Seen Myra Manes?
Studio Sidekick Is Now a Director

Manes takes the reins to direct ghost movie.

Myra Manes, the mild-mannered assistant and adviser to Moe Block Busters, was named the director of *Evilo Must Go!* after Phillip D. Rubbish unexpectedly stepped down from the project yesterday.

"I'm afraid Phillip isn't as tough as some people think," Manes said with a sly smile. "He's simply not cut out to direct a major film and run Buster Boy Entertainment."

Who is?

"Me!" said Manes, tossing her famous mane of hair over one shoulder. "I intend to direct the life out of this movie while getting the budget back on track. Just wait till Mr. Busters sees what I've done. I'm confident he'll ask me, not Phillip, to succeed him when he retires."

Moe Block Busters is scheduled to return from vacation on Friday night. Until then, Rubbish still has full authority to make major decisions for Buster Boy Entertainment.

AN EXCLUSIVE EXPOSÉ
Willie Shadow Is a Fake!
Young Actor Is Guilty of Fraud

There is no Willie Shadow. It was all a ruse cooked up by none other than Seymour Hope, 11.

In an elaborate case of fraud, Hope used the name Willie Shadow to audition for the part of Sylvester in the film *Evilo Must Go!* Since then he's been duping fans right and left.

"I have a Willie Shadow autograph," said Mary Mee. "But now I realize it's just a fake. What a rip-off!"

"I have a picture of him," said Holden Hands. "But who is he really? A liar, that's who."

Continued on page 2, column 1

FRAUD *Continued from page 1, column 2*

"I'm sorry," said Hope when asked to explain his duplicitous shenanigans. "I didn't mean to disappoint anyone. I just wanted to play myself in the movie, and I couldn't audition using my real name. That's why I made up the name Willie Shadow."

Well, that's what he claims. But who can believe *anything* Seymour Hope says?

"That kid went from hero to antihero in three weeks," said film critic Matt N. Nay. "Welcome to Hollywood."

Willie Shadow is none other than Seymour Hope, a liar.

"Grin and Bear It," Says Hollywood Dentist

At this point it's hard to say who's more frustrated with whom.

According to Ignatius B. Grumply, he's tried repeatedly to get cosmetic dentist Dr. Miles Smyle to give him a Hollywood smile—to no avail.

Now, says Grumply, he'd prefer to forget the whole thing. "I jutht want my own teeth back. Pleathe."

Smyle's response? "Oh, get over yourself. Grin and bear it."

The famous Hollywood dentist says he's tired of Grumply's complaints. "He's the most demanding patient I've ever had," said Smyle, who after

Dr. Smyle (left) says Grumply should buck up.

today's appointment is refusing to provide any additional treatment to the Ghastly author.

Feds Call Off Investigation

Officials with the Federal Aviation Administration have called off the investigation of the alleged strange phenomena on a flight last month from Ghastly, Illinois, to Los Angeles. Calling the freaky flight a "one-time fluke," officials say such oddities in the air are unlikely to happen again and should be of no concern to passengers.

MYRA MANES

PERSONAL ADVISER & ASSISTANT TO MOE BLOCK BUSTERS
BUSTER BOY ENTERTAINMENT
630 WEST 5TH STREET   LOS ANGELES, CA 90071

TO: CAST AND CREW OF *EVILO MUST GO!*

FR: MYRA MANES, DIRECTOR *MM*

RE: TOMORROW

DATE: APRIL 9

Production of *Evilo Must Go!* will finally begin tomorrow. We will start by rehearsing the climactic scene of the movie. The following characters must attend this rehearsal: Evilo, Sylvester, and Ignatius. **No other cast or crew members will be allowed on the set.**

Warning: There will be open flames, knives, explosive devices, and a live shark on set.

Rehearsal begins at 9 P.M. Miss Oscar, please be on time.

MYRA MANES

PERSONAL ADVISER & ASSISTANT TO MOE BLOCK BUSTERS
BUSTER BOY ENTERTAINMENT
630 WEST 5TH STREET   LOS ANGELES, CA 90071

DELIVERED BY COURIER

April 9

Max Schlock
Editor, *The Daily Scandal*
7721 N. Figueroa Street
Los Angeles, CA 90041

Dear Mr. Schlock,

Would you be interested in purchasing exclusive rehearsal
photos? I'm not at liberty to describe the photos just yet. But I
can tell you this: The pictures will feature Ivana Oscar in the role
of her life—and her death, if you catch my meaning.

Please let me know if you're interested in these tragic last
photos of Miss Oscar. If you are, I can deliver them to your office
late tomorrow night. The price tag is $4 million.

Helpfully yours,

Myra Manes

Myra Manes
Director, *Evilo Must Go!*

_{THE}DAILY SCANDAL

7721 N. Figueroa Street   **Los Angeles, CA 90041**

Max Schlock, Editor

April 9

Myra Manes
Buster Boy Entertainment
630 West 5th Street
Los Angeles, CA 90071

Dear Myra,

Let's see now. You're offering to sell me tragic rehearsal photos that will:

1) shock and sadden fans of Ivana Oscar so much that they'll flock to see *Evilo Must Go!* when it's released in theaters, thereby guaranteeing it'll be a major box-office hit
2) assure the late Miss Oscar a posthumous Academy Award for lifetime achievement
3) recoup the $3 million Phillip D. Rubbish lost and make an extra $1 million, thus bringing the film in under budget, and
4) sufficiently impress Moe Block Busters so that he names you (not Rubbish) to succeed him as the head of Buster Boy Entertainment

You always were a clever one, Myra. But getting the final pictures of Hollywood's favorite femme fatale? That's killer.

I'll give you the money when you deliver the pictures tomorrow night. I'll wait all night if I have to. This is my kind of story.

Scandalously yours,

Max Schlock

Max Schlock

Le Beverly Hills Hotel

"Where the Stars Stay in Style"
444 N. Rexford Drive
Beverly Hills, CA 90210

April 9

Olive C. Spence
The Cupola
43 Old Cemetery Road
Ghastly, Illinois

Dear Olive,

I owe you an apology. You were right about this whole movie business. Truth is, *I* was right at first. But then I got here and lost my senses, as did Seymour. I wish you hadn't left. Seymour needs you. The poor boy is humiliated that the tabloids are calling him a fraud and a liar. And now that we have Myra Manes as our director, I don't know what we'l

We must call a meeting, Iggy.

Olive! You're here!

Of course I'm here. Who else is going to write the final chapter of this twisted little drama?

Only you could, Olive. But I'd like to help. Seymour will want to be involved, too. Shall we meet in my room tonight?

No, let's meet in Ivana's penthouse suite. It's bigger and more comfortable. Tell Seymour to meet us there at eleven o'clock. BYOP.

BYOP?

Bring Your Own Pen. And bring a pair of pliers, too, so you can remove those ridiculous veneers from your teeth while I show you a disturbing clause in Ivana's contract.

⪻ Ivana Oscar ⪼

April 9

Dear everyone,

It seems silly to be writing when we're all gathered together here in my suite. But I do appreciate it. My hearing is so poor.

No problem, Miss Oscar. We always discuss business matters in writing. It's a rule at our house.

It's the only way I can make my ideas heard. Now, where shall we begin?

I think we need to decide how to handle tomorrow night's rehearsal. I had no idea you were in such danger, Miss Oscar, until Olive showed me that terrifying clause in your contract.

Don't worry, Miss Oscar. We won't let anybody hurt you.

I appreciate your concern, but Myra Manes is a very smart woman. If she wants me dead, I'm sure she'll find a way to have me killed legally.

Legally schmeegally. Myra is a classic villain who's driven by a ruthless desire for power. And there's one thing you have to remember about all villains.

They're all mean?

Besides that. They all have a fatal flaw. We have to determine what Myra's is.

The woman was born without a heart. Does that count?

I'm not speaking hyperbolically, Iggy. I'm asking literally, what is Myra's greatest weakness?

I'm not sure she has a weakness, Olive. She's smarter than Moe Block Busters and Phillip D. Rubbish put together. Myra has quite a brain under all that hair.

That's it! Her hair!

Seymour, you're right!

Wait. How can hair be a weakness?

Look in the mirror, Iggy. It's not just hair. It's the vanity attached to it.

Oh. I see your point. So we must attack Myra where she's most vulnerable.

Exactly. Her hair.

This is so down and dirty. In fact, it's downright evil. Or should I say, it's Evilo?

If it's Evilo they want, it's Evilo they'll get. Ivana, would you mind terribly if I played the role of the evil ghost tomorrow night?

Be my guest, Olive.

Wow! This could be even better than <u>Evilo Must Go!</u>

It will be if Olive's writing the script.

Do we need to rehearse?

No, Ivana. You just need to know your cue.

What is it?

Death clause.

Oh, I can remember that!

I know you can, dear. Now, the only thing left to do is vote. Seymour, please prepare the ballots.

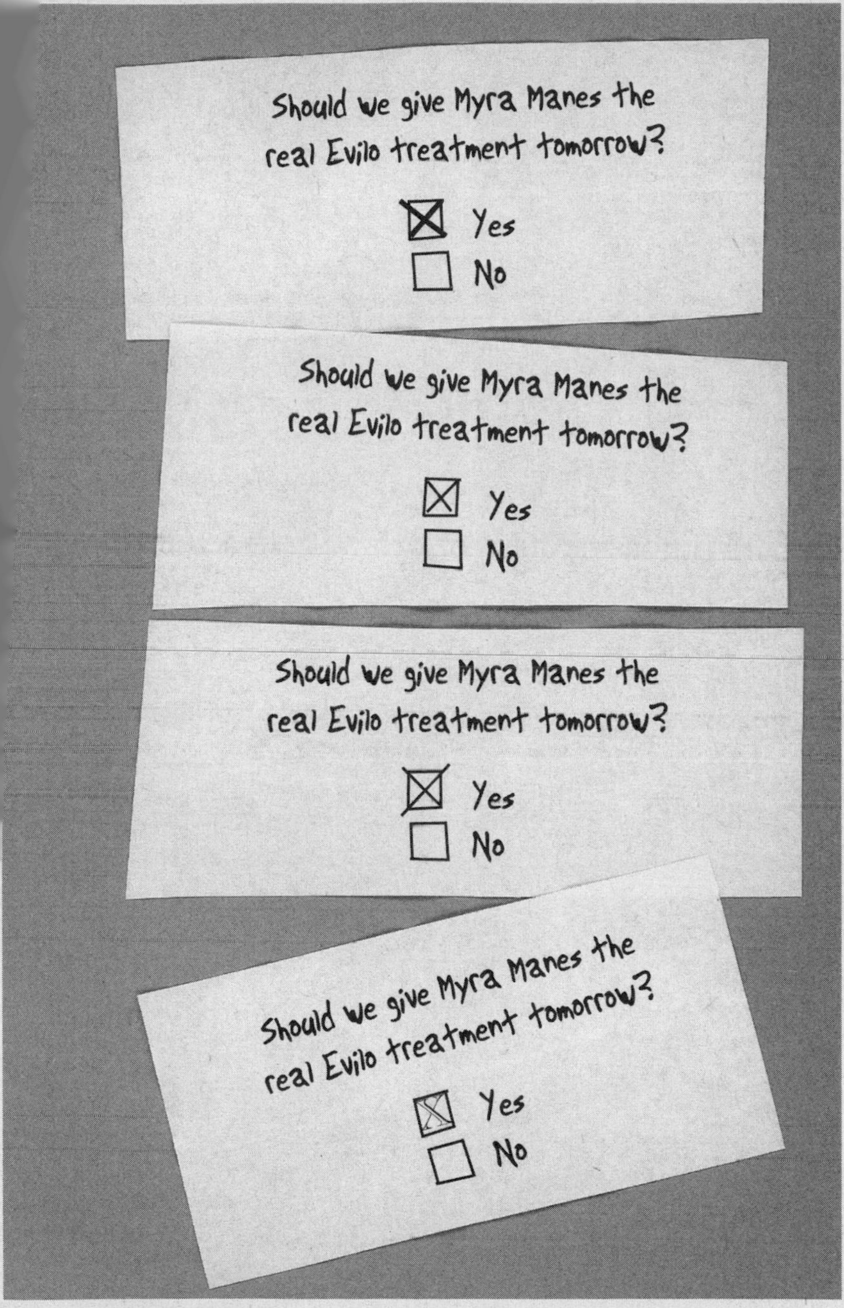
Should we give Myra Manes the real Evilo treatment tomorrow?
Yes
No
Should we give Myra Manes the real Evilo treatment tomorrow?
Yes
No
Should we give Myra Manes the real Evilo treatment tomorrow?
Yes
No
Should we give Myra Manes the real Evilo treatment tomorrow?
Yes
No

Transcript of Rehearsal
for *Evilo Must Go!*

MYRA MANES: Okay, listen up, everybody. The first stunt I want to practice is Evilo running through a burning hallway in Spence Mansion. Miss Oscar, are you ready?

IVANA OSCAR: As ready as I'll ever be.

MYRA MANES: When I say action, I want you to run as fast as you can, and I'm going to aim this flamethrower at you. It might get a little hot, but just keep running through the flames because I want to get some photos of this for, uh, marketing purposes, okay?

IVANA OSCAR: All right, dear.

MYRA MANES: Ignatius and Sylvester, stand back. Ready and . . . action! Run, Miss Oscar!

IVANA OSCAR: I'm running!

MYRA MANES: Wait a sec. My flamethrower's not working. Let's try it again. Ready and . . . action!

IVANA OSCAR: I'm running!

MYRA MANES: Wait. Ugh. Darn it. It almost
seems like someone's blowing out the flame.

IVANA OSCAR (giggling): Shall we try it
again? I'm feeling good. My muscles have
warmed up.

MYRA MANES: No, let's try the explosion
scene. This is the scene where Spence Mansion blows up. Okay, Ignatius and Sylvester, you're looking on in disbelief from
the front yard while Evilo vaporizes in a
fiery burst. Miss Oscar, I want you to . . .
Oh, crud. These explosives are soaking wet.
They were dry a minute ago. Did someone
pour water on them?

IGNATIUS B. GRUMPLY: I didn't see anyone.

MYRA MANES: Never mind. Forget it. We'll
use the shark tank. Miss Oscar, I'd like
you to climb into the shark tank.

SEYMOUR HOPE: Why would there be a shark
tank at Spence Mansion? We have a dog and
cats but not a shark.

MYRA MANES: Shut up, Sylvester. Miss Oscar,
get on that ladder and climb into the shark
tank.

IVANA OSCAR: But there's a live shark in there.

MYRA MANES: No joke, artichoke. Now get your scrawny behind up that ladder and jump into the tank with the killer shark.

IVANA OSCAR: I'm not sure I want to do that.

MYRA MANES: Oh, yeah? Well, guess what. You have to do that.

IVANA OSCAR: Why, dear?

MYRA MANES: Because of a little thing in your contract called the death clause.

[Scary music begins playing quietly as menacing claws emerge from the darkness of Spence Mansion]

MYRA MANES: Now, stop stalling, you old bat, and get in the shark tank. Why are you staring at me? And what are those creepy nails coming toward me?

IVANA OSCAR: What nails, dear?

MYRA MANES: Those five-inch fingernails floating toward me. They look like werewolf claws.

IVANA OSCAR: Oh, that's just Olive. She takes great pride in her long fingernails.

MYRA MANES: What the—? Get those creepy claws away from me! This isn't in the script. Cut! Cut!

IVANA OSCAR: Olive loves to cut. Look at Olive cut your long hair with her death claws. Cut, cut, cut! Look at her go. Olive's such a naughty ghost.

MYRA MANES: Make it stop! Stop!

IVANA OSCAR: A little vain about our hair, are we?

MYRA MANES (weakly): Please, stop! I have a weave!

IGNATIUS B. GRUMPLY: A weave? That's not your real hair?

MYRA MANES: Of course it's not my real hair! This is Hollywood. Everything's fake! I have a mild case of male-pattern baldness.

SEYMOUR HOPE (laughing): Oh my gosh!

MYRA MANES: Stop laughing, Sylvester! And stop cutting my hair, whoever you are!

IVANA OSCAR: Not until you sign on the dotted line.

MYRA MANES: What dotted line?

IGNATIUS B. GRUMPLY: Right here. It's a simple legal document that acknowledges the existence of Olive C. Spence, the ghost who's cutting your hair at this very moment.

MYRA MANES: Okay, okay. Anything to stop this haircut.

IVANA OSCAR: We'll also need Phillip's signature. Call him on your cell phone.

MYRA MANES: I'm calling, I'm calling, see? Phillip, get your [CENSORED] over here—NOW!

IVANA OSCAR: Thank you. After we get Phillip's signature, you can call the police.

MYRA MANES: The police? Why?

IVANA OSCAR: Oh, something tells me they might want a word with you, dear.

Los Angeles County Police Department

Name: Myra Manes
Height: 5'8"
Weight: 133 lbs
Special note: Partially bald
Fingerprints:

Name: Phillip D. Rubbish
Height: 6'1"
Weight: 183 lbs
Special note: Repeats himself
Fingerprints:

Warrant issued for the arrest of

Moe Block Busters

Preliminary hearings set for: Monday, April 13

THE HOLLYWOOD WHISPER

Saturday, April 11   "Movie News and Secrets You're Just *Dying* to Hear" $1.50

Evilo Directors Must Go . . . to Jail!

Manes and Rubbish are in deep doo-doo. Busters is, too.

Busters reaches for the stars, per police orders.

Myra Manes and Phillip D. Rubbish will have a lot of explaining to do when they appear in a Los Angeles courtroom on Monday.

Manes is charged with the attempted murder of Ivana Oscar. Rubbish faces conspiracy charges. Both were apprehended last night during a rehearsal for the film *Evilo Must Go!*

"Manes was trying to kill Ivana Oscar because Rubbish couldn't bring himself to do it," said Los Angeles District Attorney Mel O. Drama.

According to Drama, Moe Block Busters is facing criminal charges based on a contract he signed with Oscar that required the aging actress to die. Busters was arrested shortly after midnight at the Los Angeles International Airport.

"The evidence is clear and convincing," said Drama. "Those scoundrels were trying to make a movie to die for."

I'm just thankful the creators of *43 Old Cemetery Road* brought this matter to my attention."

Drama said he was especially grateful to Seymour Hope. "By recording last night's rehearsal on his cell phone, Seymour has made this an open-and-shut case."

Ivana Plays Dirty Hairy

Ivana Oscar has spent her career playing sultry characters on the big screen. But last night the actress played the role of a tough guy in a real-life drama that pitted her against personal assistant–turned–murderous assailant Myra Manes on the set of *Elivo Must Go!*

"I loved every minute of it!" said Oscar.

Continued on page 2, column 1

HAIRY *Continued from page 1, column 2*

The 92-year-old actress known as Hollywood's favorite femme fatale costarred with a real femme fatale, Olive C. Spence.

"Olive has been dead since 1911," said Oscar. "But she played her part with such energy and life. It was an inspiration!"

The scene involved the invisible Spence cutting Myra Manes's hair with a pair of clawlike artificial fingernails.

"Olive found the claws in a prop room," said Oscar, giggling. "They were from an old werewolf movie, but we called them the death claws. Olive says she was inspired by the death clause in my contract. Oh, you should have seen those claws circling Myra

Oscar (left) says she enjoyed acting tough with Spence (right).

and snipping away at her hair. We had no idea it was a hairpiece, but that only made the scene better. It was a perfect Hollywood moment made possible by a terrific script, great acting and the most delicious bit of good luck."

"We Own Moe!"
Clever Creators of *43 Old Cemetery Road* Now Own Buster Boy Entertainment

Brilliant. Masterful. A dose of their own bad medicine.

That's how legal experts are describing the contracts Myra Manes and Phillip D. Rubbish signed late last night. The clever contracts were written by Ignatius B. Grumply.

"I had to get Myra Manes to acknowledge the existence of Olive," explained Grumply. "That way, the contract I signed with Moe Block Busters is null and void because it doesn't bear the signature of the legal coauthor of *43 Old Cemetery Road*, namely Olive C. Spence."

But perhaps the craftier contract was the one Grumply convinced Rubbish to sign. "I knew Phillip had the authority to sign contracts for Moe Block Busters," said Grumply. "So I simply had Phillip transfer Buster Boy Entertainment over to us. Now we own Moe."

Hope and Grumply take five.

Grumply said he, Spence and Hope have already asked Ivana Oscar to manage their new film studio.

"I'm going to do it!" said Oscar. "Why not? I have more experience than anyone in this town, and I'm not planning on dying anytime soon."

Continued on page 3, column 1

OWN *Continued from page 2, column 2*

The new owners said they plan to rename the movie studio Majority Rules Entertainment, based on their method of making business decisions.

Hope was involved in all the business decisions, though his name does not appear on any of the contracts.

"I'm too young to sign legal documents," said the disappointed 11-year-old. "And my dad still won't let me see grown-up movies. Talk about a crime."

Smyle, Ahtmee Charged with Crimes

Hollywood's favorite dentist (left) and stylist (right) are in hot water.

Smiles by the miles? Maybe.

Or maybe those pearly white porcelain veneers were really crocodile smiles.

Investigators say they believe that Dr. Miles Smyle was using teeth from crocodiles to produce the Hollywood smiles that made him famous.

"How else am I supposed to give my patients the humungous smiles they want?" asked Smyle in an incriminating interview with police.

Authorities are studying the veneers Ignatius B. Grumply recently removed from his own teeth.

In other news, Hollywood stylist Luke Ahtmee has been charged with crimes against fashion for the image makeovers he performed on Ignatius Grumply and Seymour Hope last month.

Scandal's Schlock Caught with Shocking Headline

Schlock is shocked.

Max Schlock, editor of the *Daily Scandal*, has a scandal all his own today. The tabloid titan was discovered in his office last night with a front-page mock-up that read: "IVANA SAY GOOD-BYE! Shocking Photos of Ivana Oscar's Final Minutes!"

"It's obvious that Schlock had full knowledge of the plan to murder Ivana Oscar," said Los Angeles District Attorney Mel O. Drama. "If Schlock's trashy tabloid is one casualty of this whole sordid affair, I for one will not shed a tear."

Really, It's *Fine*

The Federal Aviation Administration (FAA) issued another bulletin yesterday to remind air travelers that flying is safe.

"Whatever happened on that flight from Ghastly, Illinois, to Los Angeles a month ago was a fluke," said FAA spokesman Don Worrie. "It won't happen again, I promise."

To assure worried passengers, Worrie plans to fly roundtrip from Ghastly to Los Angeles on Monday.

Hundreds of celebrity handprints, footprints, and autographs are set in concrete in front of Grauman's Chinese Theatre on Hollywood Boulevard.

Hi, everybody! Sorry we didn't become movie stars. Guess it wasn't in the stars for us. We'll be home soon!
    Love,

        —Seymour

URGENT

The Ghastly Times
20 Scary Street
Ghastly, Illinois

The famous Hollywood Sign, a legendary
symbol of American movies, was erected in
1923 to promote a real estate development.

Dear neighbors,

Hollywood was a bust, but at
least we got a good story out
of it. See you soon. I'm eager
to admire the improvements
to Spence Mansion.

Kind regards,
Ignatius B. Grumply

POST CARD

URGENT

The Ghastly Times
20 Scary Street
Ghastly, Illinois

Dear friends,

It seems like we've been gone
forever. I'm eager to see you
all again. We're bringing a
friend to visit. I know you'll
like her!

Until very soon,

Olive

P.S. Wish me luck flying
home. The trip out here was
most unpleasant.

POST CARD

URGENT

The Ghastly Times
20 Scary Street
Ghastly, Illinois

32¢

USA

Los Angeles
CA
PM
APRIL 11

➤THE GHASTLY TIMES◄

Tuesday, April 14
Cliff Hanger, Editor

"We're Living in Ghastly Times"

50 cents
Morning Edition

Welcome Home!

All of Ghastly turned out last night to greet Ignatius B. Grumply, Olive C. Spence and Seymour Hope after their month in Hollywood.

"There's no place like home," said Hope, who was delighted by the combination welcome-home party and surprise birthday party that awaited him at Spence Mansion. Locals were awed by the sight of screen legend Ivana Oscar, who arrived in Ghastly with the Spence Mansion residents.

"We were thrilled that Miss Oscar accepted our invitation to visit," said Grumply. "She's become a wonderful friend of our family. I know everyone will enjoy getting to know her. Also, before I forget, we wanted to thank M. Balm for caring for our pets. And if I could find Hugh Briss, I'd like to thank him for making repairs to Spence Mansion while we

The bestselling trio returns home with a new friend.

were gone. Has anyone seen Mr. Briss? I owe him five hundred dollars."

"No, you don't," said Balm.

(See story below.)

Hugh Briss Led to His Own Downfall

Hugh Briss is now in stable condition at Greater Ghastly Memorial Hospital. It's a far cry from where he was last Friday: lying in agony on the sidewalk in front of Spence Mansion after a dramatic fall from the cupola.

"I was trying to replace a few broken tiles," Briss explained. "Looking back, I guess I should've used a harness or hired an assistant. But I didn't think I needed any help. I thought I could do it myself. I thought I could do everything with one hand tied behind my back."

Continued on page 2, column 1

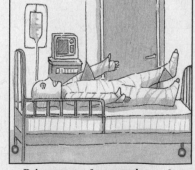

Briss recovers from cupola oopala.

BRISS *Continued from page 1, column 1*

That's what Briss believed—until he lost his footing and fell off the cupola, breaking nearly every bone in his body. Doctors say Briss will be in a body cast for at least six months.

Librarian M. Balm said he was sad but not surprised to hear the news. "I hate to say it, but Hugh Briss led to his own downfall."

Happy Birthday, Seymour!

Seymour Hope celebrated his twelfth birthday last night with cake, music and gifts from family and friends.

Olive C. Spence and Ignatius B. Grumply gave their son an antique Kinetoscope and a modern movie camera. "Seymour did such a terrific job shooting our rehearsal on his cell phone," said Grumply. "Olive and I thought he should try making a movie with a professional camera. Besides, we made him leave the cell phone in California."

Perhaps the most dramatic gift came from none other than Ivana Oscar, who asked Seymour if he'd be interested in being her adopted grandson.

"Miss Oscar said I already have the best mom and dad in the world," said Hope. "But she wondered if I'd like a grandmother. Of course I said yes. She also wants me to direct her next movie." (See side story.)

Hope is surprised by party and gifts.

Hope to Direct *Hollywood, Dead Ahead*

Hope will direct Oscar in new film.

Seymour Hope will direct Ivana Oscar in *Hollywood, Dead Ahead,* a film based on the latest chapters in the serialized novel *43 Old Cemetery Road.* It will be the first movie produced by Majority Rules Entertainment.

"It's the true story of our recent trip to California," said Oscar. "We'll all play ourselves in the movie. I think Seymour will do a wonderful job directing. I'm just sorry I got him in trouble with that whole stage-name business."

Seymour said he wasn't angry with Miss Oscar. "I never would've been chosen to play the part of Sylvester if I hadn't used a fake name," he said. "And if I hadn't gotten the part, I never would've seen the downside of fame. I'm glad we're all finally going to be in a movie together. I'm also super excited to make a movie for kids like me who aren't allowed to see R-rated movies."

Hollywood, Dead Ahead will be the first film to carry the GG rating.

"It stands for ghost or granny guidance suggested," said Hope, who hopes the film is the first of many such projects. "After this I want to make *Evilo and the Death Claws, Death Claws 2* and then *Return of the Death Claws.*"

"Heaven help us," said his father with a heavy sigh.

FAA Reopens Investigation

Floating suitcases. Flying opera glasses. A pastrami sandwich that disappeared bite by bite.

These were just a few of the things seen and heard on a flight yesterday from Los Angeles to Ghastly. In response, the Federal Aviation Administration (FAA) has reopened its investigation of strange phenomena on domestic flights.

"I was on that flight," said Don Worrie, spokesman for the FAA. "Believe me, there was definitely something weird going on."

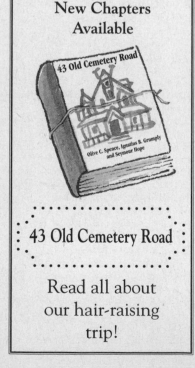

And that's how this story ends.
The residents of Spence Mansion
are back home,

Home, Haunted Home

Hope Grows Here

Laughter Is the Best Medicine

where they have pets to pamper,
a film to focus on,
delicious meals and books to make,
and, of course, letters to read and write.

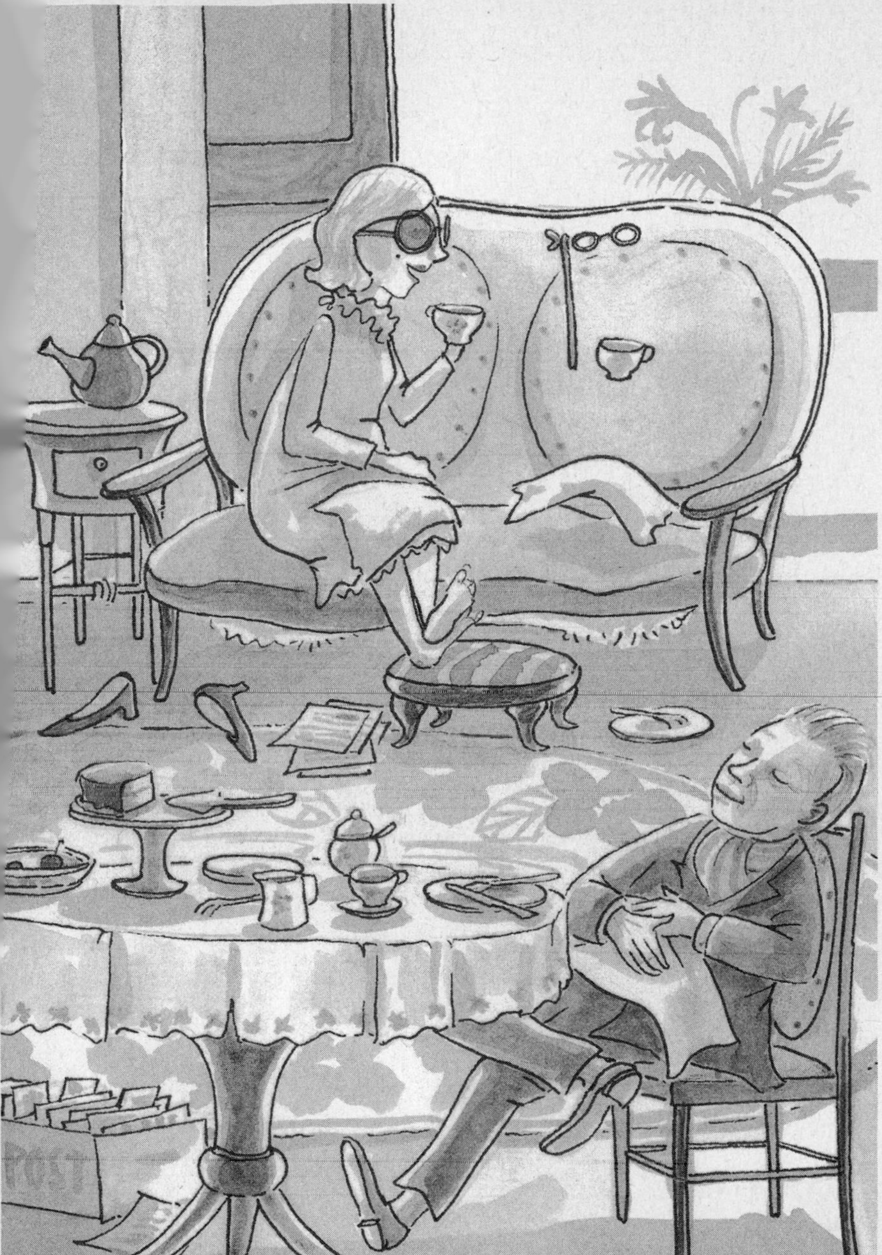

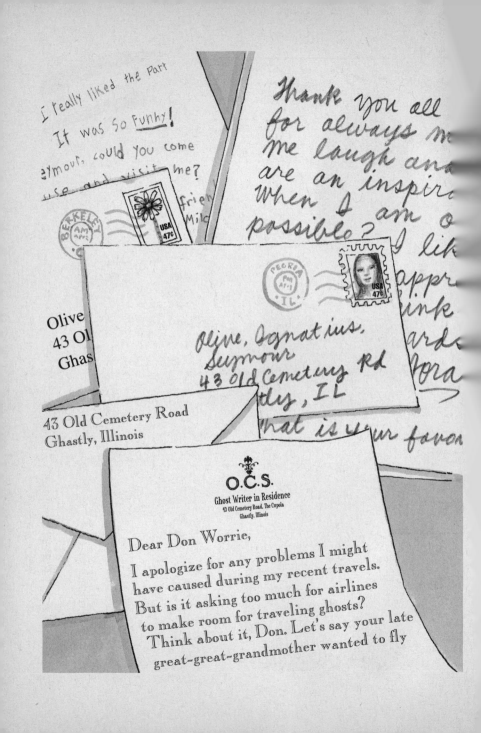

I really liked the Part
It was so Funny!
...eymour, could you come
...use and visit me?
frien...
Mild...

Thank you all
for always m...
me laugh and
are an inspir...
When I am o...
possible? I lik...
appr...
ink...
ard...
ora...
...nat is your favor...

BERKELEY
CA
AM
APR...

PEORIA
PM
APR...
IL

USA
47¢

Olive...
43 Ol...
Ghas...

Olive, Ignatius,
Seymour
43 Old Cemetery Rd
...tly, IL

43 Old Cemetery Road
Ghastly, Illinois

O.C.S.
Ghost Writer in Residence
43 Old Cemetery Road, The Cupola
Ghastly, Illinois

Dear Don Worrie,

I apologize for any problems I might
have caused during my recent travels.
But is it asking too much for airlines
to make room for traveling ghosts?
Think about it, Don. Let's say your late
great-great-grandmother wanted to fly

And let's not forget everyone's favorite femme fatale,
who feels twenty, no, *fifty* years younger
than she did one hundred pages ago.

If you listen very closely,
you just might hear
Ivana Oscar
practicing a speech
she will deliver in the
not-too-distant future.

I'd like to thank the members of the Academy

for this lovely award,

which would not have been possible without the

help of

my dear friend and director,

Seymour Hope,

who gave me the best advice of my life

when he told me

that as long as I'm laughing,

I'll be a kid forever.

Thank you. Thank you. Thank you!

Should we end the story here?

☒ Yes
☐ No

Should we end the story here?

☒ Yes
☐ No

Should we end the story here?

☒ Yes
☐ No

Should we end the story here?

☒ Yes
☐ No

But let's write more later!

The End
for now

Kisses, darlings!

ACKNOWLEDGMENTS

We would like to thank everyone
who made this book possible,
including
our friends,
our family,
our publisher,
and all the people
who read our books.
Yes, *you* are the reason
we do what we do.
So deep bows to you, gentle reader.
You're the real
STAR
of this show.

Your devoted fans,

Kate and *Sarah*

Author **Kate Klise** (left) and illustrator **M. Sarah Klise** (right) grew up in Peoria, Illinois, where they spent many summers making home movies with their beloved aunt, actress Mariclare Costello Arbus. Under her direction, the Klise sisters and their siblings wrote and acted in rollicking renditions of popular tales, such as "Cinderella" and "Hansel and Gretel." (For pivotal scenes, the Klises even went in costume to a local bank and restaurant!)

Kate now watches movies at her home in Norwood, Missouri. Sarah sees films near her house in Berkeley, California. They hope their aunt enjoys this book. For more about the Klise sisters, visit **www.kateandsarahklise.com**.

**Other books written by Kate Klise
and illustrated by M. Sarah Klise:**

Dying to Meet You: 43 Old Cemetery Road (Book One)
Over My Dead Body: 43 Old Cemetery Road (Book Two)
Till Death Do Us Bark: 43 Old Cemetery Road (Book Three)
The Phantom of the Post Office: 43 Old Cemetery Road (Book Four)
Greetings from the Graveyard: 43 Old Cemetery Road (Book Six)

Regarding the Fountain
Regarding the Sink
Regarding the Trees
Regarding the Bathrooms
Regarding the Bees

The Show Must Go On: Three-Ring Rascals (Book One)
Letters from Camp
Trial by Journal

Shall I Knit You a Hat?
Why Do You Cry?
Imagine Harry
Little Rabbit and the Night Mare
Little Rabbit and the Meanest Mother on Earth
Stand Straight, Ella Kate
Grammy Lamby and the Secret Handshake

Also written by Kate Klise:

Deliver Us from Normal
Far from Normal
Grounded
Homesick
In the Bag

Don't Miss This Ghastly Whodunit!

Greetings from the Graveyard
43 Old Cemetery Road: Book Six

Roses are red,
Violets are blue.
If a ghost can write books,
Why not greeting cards, too?

The bestselling trio from Spence Mansion—Ignatius B. Grumply, Olive C. Spence, and Seymour Hope—are launching a greeting-card company called Greetings from the Graveyard.

But what kind of card do you send to an ex-girlfriend who threatens to publish the love letters of Ignatius B. Grumply? And what do you send when the town of Ghastly is rocked by its first crime wave and two escaped convicts are on the loose?

If you're Olive C. Spence, you send for your old butler, T. Leeves, who arrives just in time for tea—and trouble!

Books are read,
Cards are, too.
Like to laugh?
This one's for you!

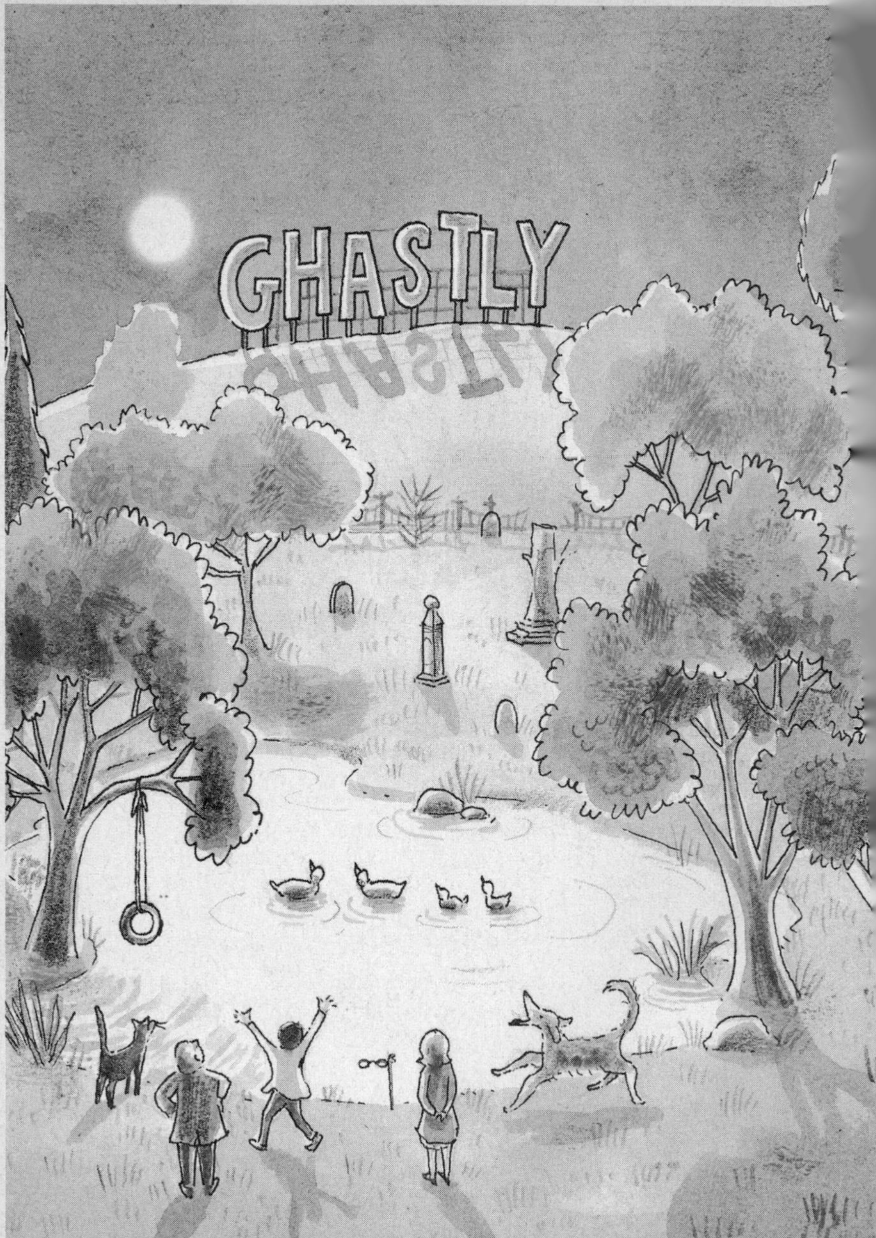
GHASTLY

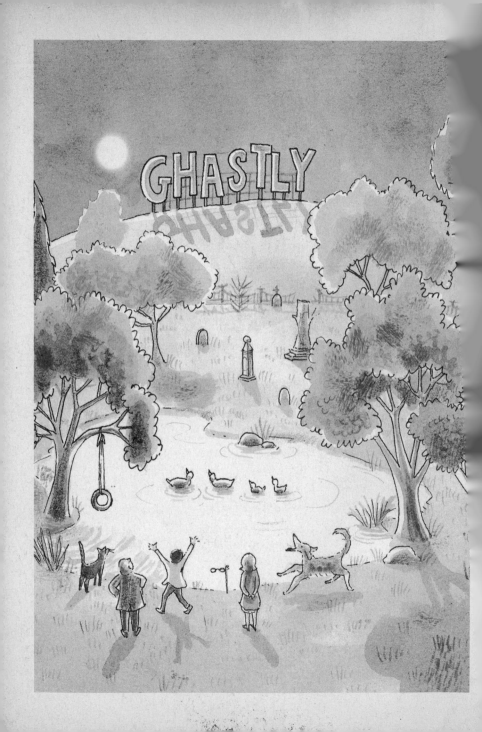

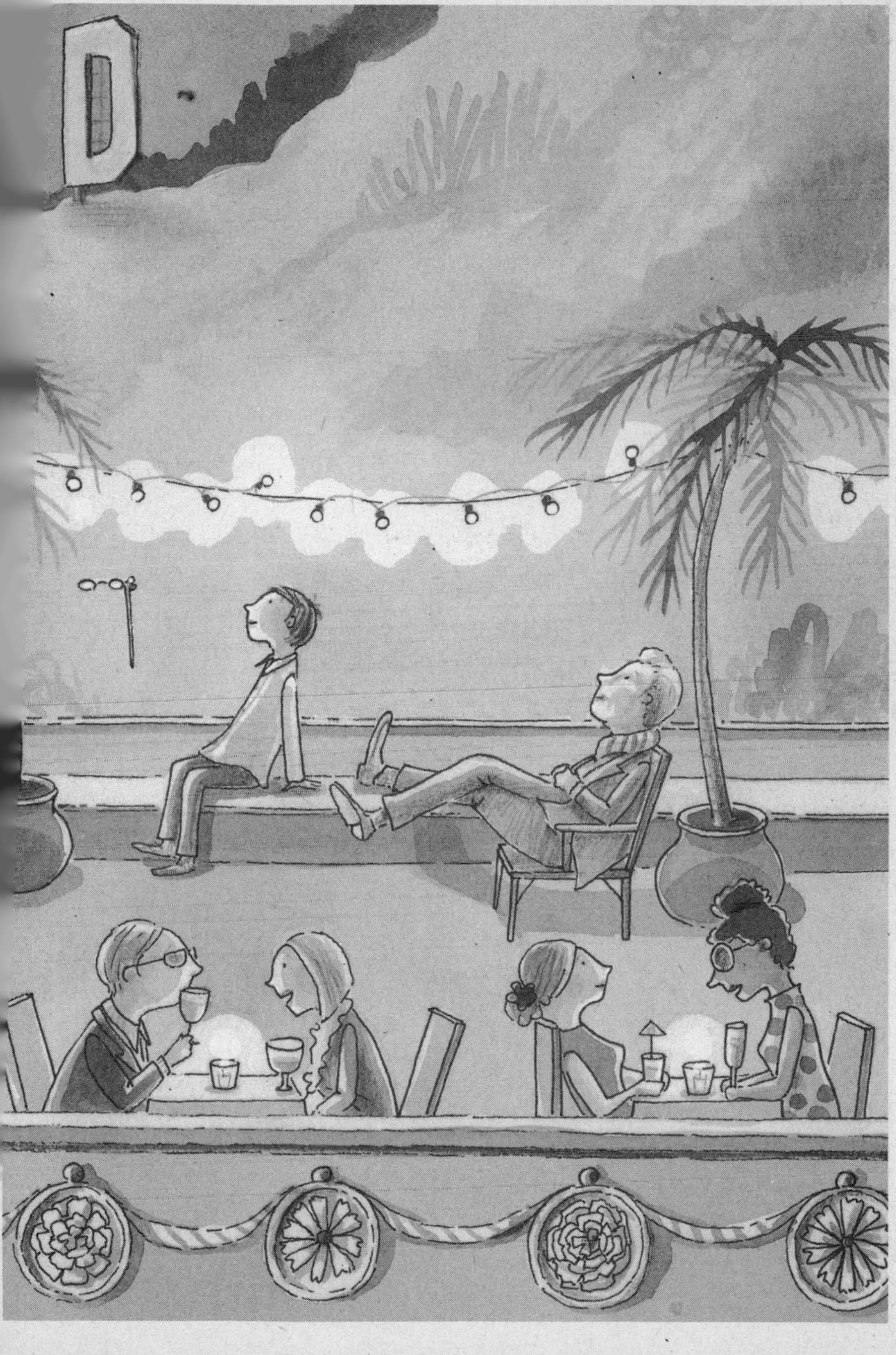